The New Gold Rush

Jon Amsden

© 2010

Ocean Park Press
Santa Monica, California

Ocean Park Press

1219 Ocean Park Boulevard
Santa Monica, CA 90405

(310) 452-2865

Book design by Robert R. Shrestha

ISBN 978-0-9828533-0-6

Table of Contents

Foreword

Money is something that all of us think about a lot. However we don't usually think about it in an analytical way. If a visitor from Mars were to ask us how money works and why we worry about it a lot, we could answer the second question fairly easily, but the first one might just leave us scratching our heads. This is one of the problems that had to be faced in writing this book. After spending a fair amount of time trying to find an answer to that first question, I finally had to admit that there is no logical proof that shows clearly why money does the job that we want it to do and why it some times fails us in a number of respects. Money is a medium of exchange, a unit of account, and a store of value. Fine! But there are any number of things that you can't buy with money (love for example). There are many things that money cannot really measure (like the cost of a giant oil spill). Most important, however, is probably the fact that sometimes money can fail to retain its value in the way we want and expect it to. What anyone trying to explain the past, to evaluate the present, or to predict the future when the topic of money is on the table is eventually faced with is that the only kind of explanation of the mystery and magic of money that even begins to approach a satisfactory analysis is an historical one.

Consequently, along with some very practical advice about why to buy, when to by, and how to buy one of the oldest forms of money (gold), the reader will find a lot of history in the following chapters. There simply isn't any other way to do it, not even for people who love mathematical equations. Fortunately I had some help in my efforts in this respect. For this I must thank my fellow University of London graduate Professor Hajinder Singh, B.A., M.Sc. for some valuable suggestions that he made that were incorporated in the manuscript. I am also deeply indebted to my dear friend A.R. Ellis, an astute market analyst and tireless reader of almost everything, for many years of daily conversations during which I learned most of what I know about how markets actually work. The principal questions that animate every chapter that follows have to do with the way that gold has been and continues to be related to the money that we use every day, and whether or not the prudent individual should place some quantity of humankind's oldest form of money aside to deal with the emergencies that the world economy and international events may have in store.

Introduction: A Barbarous Relic

In the midst of one his many discussions of the dynamics of the free market capitalist system and its tendency to break down on occasions, the British economist John Maynard Keynes referred to gold as a "barbarous relic."

J.M. Keynes' "Barbarous Relic"

This remark dates to a time when Keynes was expending his considerable intellectual and polemical energy to oppose the sober and restrictive nature of the so-called "gold standard" which dominated international economic life throughout most of the 19th Century. When, however, it was necessary to re-order the economies of the free market nations after World War II, and while the victors of the Second World War were, therefore, planning the post-war world economic order at a mountain resort in Bretton Woods, New Hampshire, Keynes was very careful to insure that the currencies of the forty-four nations represented at the conference would all be linked to gold at the rate of $35 US dollars per ounce.

When the gold price finally broke through the $1000 /oz. level late in 2009, therefore, it seemed a good time to revisit the ancient arguments about gold and money. Probably the most important reason for doing this would be to imagine what might happen if, at some point in the future, the US dollar should collapse under the weight of incredible amounts of US debt both foreign and domestic. One possibility is that if/when this were to happen the inflation that followed would cause the price of gold to head for the stratosphere. Let's take a look at gold itself to see why this particular member of the Periodic Chart seems to have been chosen by history to play such an important role in the creation of currencies, the preservation of wealth, and the processes of international trade.

Gold's closest neighbors on the Periodic Chart are Platinum, Palladium, Silver, and Mercury. Unlike these metals, however, gold is almost entirely chemically inert. This is why gold bars found in the wreck of , for example, a Spanish Galleon are retrieved from the bottom of the sea in perfect shape with not so much as a scrap of seaweed to hide the glitter. It is not, however, gold's atomically incorruptible nature that causes this almost magical substance to be so highly valued. Probably more important is the fact that when gold is found in a stream bed or in an underground rock seam it can be retrieved in an almost chemically pure state. For this reason, gold was one of the first metals found, worked into jewelry, coins, and bars, and hence treasured by the rich and powerful throughout human history. The mythical Golden Fleece, so painfully acquired by Jason and his Argonauts, was created by one of the first methods of collecting this shiny and imperishable metal. A sheep skin was weighted down in a stream that flowed near gold bearing strata. What then happened was that the lanolin impregnated wool of the sheep would capture and hold tiny particles of gold borne by the water flowing through it.

It was not, however, because gold was relatively easily separated from the bosom of Mother Earth that it became the object of the frenzied 19th Century "gold rushes" as well as the motive for theft and murder through most of human history. The reason for gold's high status among the metals is actually due to its relative scarcity. While gold is easier than, for example, silver to separate from the minerals that encase it, there is much less gold in the Earth's mantle than most other metals. What this means, of course, is that gold requires a great labor of searching, washing, and collecting to amass even a tiny portion of the stuff. As we shall see, it is precisely gold's character of requiring massive amounts of human activity to locate, to mine and to transport it from the farthest corners of the Earth that makes gold an emperor among the metals.

The theory that will be used to explain gold's high place among the precious metals in the chapters that follow will be one that is based on the assumption that it is people at work who are, somehow, the source of all economic value. This theory has a very long history. Although the Muslim polymath Ibin Khaldun (1332-1406) may have been the first to point out in his *Muquaddima* (1377) that it is the labor of human beings alone that creates wealth, it is to the Englishman William Petty (1623-1687) that the first clear statement of this idea is usually attributed. Petty was a man who rose from relatively humble beginnings. In a long and varied life Petty studied medicine in Amsterdam, hobnobbed (pun intended) with the eminent and equally exiled Thomas Hobbes (1588-1679) in Paris, and then (changing sides) served as the Chief Physician to Thomas Cromwell's armies in Ireland. Later, however, Petty changed sides again to become the loyal statistician and chief economist for Charles II (1630-1685) in Restoration England. In this last mentioned capacity, Petty (now Sir William Petty) wrote his *Treatise of Taxes and Contributions* (1692) in which work he attributed the creation of all wealth to "land and labour."

It was, however, the young colonial polymath Benjamin Franklin who, at the age of 23, made the first politically pointed use of the labor theory of value. Following basic mercantilist concepts, the rulers in the imperial homeland had subjected their north American subjects to the most restrictive monetary regime imaginable. The "colonials" were simply not allowed to use the British coinage. Neither were the British residents of North America allowed to mint their own coins. A New England mint that provided a copper coinage for small change was told to close, operating a mint being a Royal privilege. To oppose this Draconian monetary regime, the young Franklin wrote a pamphlet in which he sang the praises of paper money for use in his "province" and, as is explained in greater detail in Chapter 5 of this book, based his argument squarely on the idea that it was those who labored who created wealth. The Englishman Petty may have collected the apples, but it was Benjamin Franklin who made the labor theory of value as American as apple pie.

Although the Scottish grandfather of economic theory, Adam Smith

(1723-1790), did not recognize any debt to Benjamin Franklin in the realm of political economy, it is nevertheless the case that Smith knew Franklin personally, and made use of at least some of Franklin's publications in his masterpiece of political economy entitled *Enquiry Into the Nature and Causes of the Wealth of Nations* (1776). In this work, as we shall see, Adam Smith made a simple and straightforward version of the labor theory of value the foundation stone of his still widely admired economic theory.

In this respect, Smith was followed by David Ricardo (1772-1783). Ricardo was a sometime member of Parliament and a shrewd economic actor in his own right. Ricardo used an expanded and improved version of the labor theory of value to advocate the repeal of Britain's Corn Laws (1815-1846)- much to the dissatisfaction of the increasingly wealthy British aristocracy of his day who had profited from the Napoleonic adventure on the continent of Europe by enjoying the first truly generous governmental support for national agriculture.

The German Doctor of Philosophy and immigrant Karl Marx (1818-1883), who cheerfully pointed to David Ricardo as his "master", put the final touches on the labor theory of value while, at the same time, giving this theory his own radical political slant. Marx regarded gold to be a "universal commodity." What he meant by this was that gold was unique among all other commodities (i.e., goods produced for sale) in that all the other commodities to be found in the marketplace could be priced in gold. It was this "universal commodity" quality of our mysterious metal that caused Marx to treat gold itself as "money" and as a substance that must be linked to all other forms of money in some intimate and indestructible way.

What will become clear in the first few pages of the chapter that follows is that, in human history, money begins as commodities. Although the list of commodity monies offered in Chapter 1 includes a long and amazing number of everyday items used as money, what the evolution of the world economy through time shows is that gold and silver played ever more dominant roles as commodity monies down through the millennia. This was especially true after the invention of coinage in a country called Lydia in the 6th Century BCE. As we shall see, stamping certain quantities of precious metal with the image and the promises of a political ruler vastly facilitated market activities wherever it was done. The historical result was that the creation of coinage accelerated economic growth in one region of the ancient world after another.

More recently, with the industrial revolution and the creation of the various European empires that followed, money as a medium of exchange, a unit of account, and a store of value expanded its' economic role far beyond the abilities of the ancient systems of metal coinage. It was the next iteration of the monetary miracle, namely paper money, that would meet the needs of trade in an ever-expanding world economy. In the first instance paper money was, most probably, a "promise to pay" carried from one banker to another by a ship captain who was doing business in a distant port. However, national banking systems using "promises to pay" came along in short order.

From the earliest days of money as paper, what was passed from hand to hand was called "representative money." Thus, the paper money in use in the advanced industrial countries, for example during the operation of the 19th Century international gold standard, simply "represented" a certain amount of gold that was being guarded in a banker's vault somewhere. To obtain the gold itself, the bearer of paper money had merely to visit the bank in question and to exchange the note for gold coins. Later, however, due to the stresses and strains of world war and revolution, money reached its final (and almost fictional) state. What was called "fiat money" did not (does not) guarantee its bearer anything at all except the exchange of the note in hand for another note just like it. The fiat money system worked reasonably well within nations but not so well between nations. For international trade, and this has been true throughout the greatest part of economic history, the eventual exchange of actual physical gold was required to balance the books.

The gold standard worked well for international trade in the 19th Century, but broke down during the mass destruction and consequent interruption of international trade caused by two World Wars. The gold standard for international trade was, however, revived after World War II. This occurred at a conference held near Bretton Woods, New Hampshire in 1944. On this occasion, the gold standard was, once again, established for international trade. This was accomplished by linking no less than 44 national currencies to gold through the intermediary of the US dollar. It was on this occasion that the brilliant and intellectually forceful John Maynard Keynes forgot about his disapproval of the "barbarous relic", and used his considerable powers of persuasion to re-create an ingenious form of the gold standard to be used in the commerce between nations.

Later, however, US President Richard M. Nixon ended the last formal link between the American dollar and gold when he "shut the gold window" of the US Treasury in 1971 in a unilateral action that soon became known around the world as "the Nixon shock." Very shortly after taking this step, however, the US President seems to have made a very interesting arrangement with the rulers of Saudi Arabia. In exchange for a promise of military protection by the United States, and first-in-line status for buying American arms, the Saudi Royal family promised Nixon that, henceforth, Saudi Arabia would accept only the US dollar in exchange for their petroleum. What this meant was that the US dollar once again became- in a somewhat restricted, but very real way -a commodity backed currency. The OPEC oil embargo that began in the following year probably delayed the full impact of the Nixon/Saudi secret agreement, but even during the world-wide petroleum shortage that followed, the price of oil continued to be quoted in US dollars. Once the crisis had passed, the "petrodollar" continued to strengthen its position as an international reserve currency and as the basic international unit of value- a role that continued unchallenged until very recently.

It will be maintained in the following chapters of this book that one of the many things that may come to challenge the dollar's domestic strength and international role in times of economic turbulence yet to come, will be our magic mystery metal gold. So as to demonstrate this in the clearest possible way, the whole enigmatic and fascinating tale of gold and money will be approached both in terms of its historical development and in the categories of monetary analysis. Telling the story of gold and money in this way will be carried out with a view towards providing a practical guide for investing in gold markets today. What will be developed in Chapters 2, 4, 6, 8 and

10 that follow will be the answers to the questions that many people have about buying gold. This will be followed by a basic description of gold markets and how they work. The information developed in this way will , hopefully, be of considerable interest to readers who, in times of global economic chaos, feel the need to understand the relationships between gold, money, and the future of our economy, in increasingly troubled times.

Chapter I   Metals and Money

Anyone reading this book will have three major questions in mind from the moment they turn this page. These are: 1) Why should I buy gold?; 2) When should I buy gold?; and finally, 3) How should I buy gold? To these three questions could be added one more. Why don't I buy some other expensive item whose value will resist the inflation that may be coming our way- diamonds for example? As many sophisticated market operators from John Maynard Keynes through Warren Buffet have observed, there is something that boggles the mind about the human fascination with gold. This may be due to the fact that there is something quite contrary to our sense of logic about digging a deep hole in the earth in South Africa to find gold which, once mined and refined, is deposited deep in the earth once again, this time beneath a London bank.

The first three of these questions will be answered in specific detail in chapters 2, 4, and 6 that follow. However to answer that last question will require a historical analysis that will range from ancient times down to the present, and will take up all of the other chapters of this book. What we shall learn by looking back on the evolution of the twin phenomena- gold and money -is this. The reason that people have struggled to acquire gold since ancient times is because gold is money, and money is what is needed to buy and sell the items that we need in the course of our daily lives. The reason that gold is money is not- as you may have already guessed -a purely logical one. On the contrary, the best way to understand why gold is money (and how gold is related to other types of money) is by looking at its history. We shall begin a quick review of that history now.

The Evolution of Money from Cocoa Beans to Zeros and Ones

Gold items are found in archeological sites in many parts of the world. Among these fascinating finds are the remains of gold jewelry dating from the Chalcolithic (i.e., copper) age of the 4th Millennium BCE. These were discovered in an archeological site called "Varna" in what is today Bulgaria. In that far off period, copper was the chief metal of tools and weapons and the precious metals were used largely for decoration.

In a period much closer to recorded history, the Anatolian poet Homer sang of the decision not to fight taken by the wealthy Trojan Prince Hector and the giant Greek warrior Ajax. In Homer's great epic poem *The Iliad* Hector said:

> *Let us give each other gifts, unforgettable gifts,*

so any man may say, Trojan soldier or Argive,
'First they fought with heart-devouring hatred,
then they parted, bound by pacts of friendship.'
With that he gave him his silver-studded sword,
slung in its sheath in a supple well-cut sword strap,
and Ajax gave his war-belt glistening purple.[1]

In later times, however, gold and other metals (including copper) became even more useful than the bronze used in Hector's sword or in the spear point with which Achilles finally laid Hector low. After being used in weapons and armor, metals of all kinds entered human history in a much more significant way. This was through the process of becoming money.

The use of the precious and semi-precious metals as commodity money, of course, came at the end of a long parade of many other useful and/or valuable items that were used for this purpose. Such items included the carefully cut and arranged parts of seashells called "wampum" that Peter Stuyvesant borrowed in great numbers to fund the creation of his New Amsterdam citadel; the cocoa beans that the Aztecs and their subjects used both to pay tribute to Montezuma as well as to buy a fat turkey on market day; and, the full measures of barley (*shekels*) that became the means of exchange and the unit of account in the cities of Mesopotamia certainly two and perhaps even three millennia before the present era.

---

[1] Fagels, Robert, Trans., *The Iliad*, Homer, New York: Viking Penguin, 1990, *p.224.*

18

Commodities like these, some of which turned out to be even more convenient than baskets of barley or handfuls of cocoa beans, included a long list of objects of daily use. Such forms of commodity money included both the sort of mundane objects that one might expect to see utilized in familiar ways such as agricultural products (e.g., rice, cows, and coconuts) as well as a number of somewhat more unusual items including cowry shells, turkey quills filled with gold dust, and slave girls. Whether as common as the daily bowl of gruel or as unusual as a very large plate of pure copper (used in Sweden), all of the forms of commodity money that history has recorded were used to facilitate the following functions of economic life:

- to pay for purchases;
- to assign the value of anything that might be purchased;
- or, to be withdrawn from market activity and saved for a rainy day.

Money, as most of the following examples will show, has always been invested with an enigmatic sort of power. Why does it work? When does it fail? And how, exactly, did it make its long journey through human history? As we shall see, money's long, and even sometimes quite bizarre, evolutionary pathway began with what is usually called "commodity money." This is money in the guise of something that is useful, edible, has magic power, or is even simply beautiful and which, therefore, can always be kept by those who possess it for their own enjoyment and as a permanent addition to their personal wealth.

There are, of course, surprising examples of commodity money that are not particularly useful or edible, and which seem to possess the only the third quality of money mentioned above-namely its ability to act as a store of value. Milton Friedman, in his book entitled *Money Mischief,* leads off his list of mischievous monetary phenomena with the tale of the Yap islanders in the South Pacific. This happy island people used giant wheels of stone called *"fei"* as a store of wealth. Quarried many miles away from the villages of Yap, and measuring in some cases as much as twelve feet in diameter, *fei* conferred an aura of wealth upon their owners, Friedman says, even when resting at the bottom of the sea.[2]

On the more useful side, it is possible to point to the example of a form of commodity money that was once based on a pound of cured tobacco. This was the "tobacco money" that developed spontaneously in the Chesapeake Bay region of early colonial North America. The "tobacco currency" was developed by the early English cultivators of this highly addictive substance by making a standard weight of tobacco acceptable as a unit of currency. The tobacco currency was in use for many years in the region that became Virginia and Maryland. It was also a form of commodity money that, very early in life, moved

---

[2] Friedman, Milton, *Money Mischief.* New York: Harcourt Brace Jovanovich, 1992. p.4.

on to the next stage in the evolution of money. The next stage was reached by moving up a notch in terms of convenience and acceptability by the simple device of becoming a paper currency. The tobacco notes that passed from hand to hand in the Chesapeake Bay region were obviously much more convenient to take to market, or to hand over to anxious creditors, than bundles of recently cured tobacco. [3]

Rather than pass lumps of tobacco from hand to hand, the early English colonists of the region simply used pieces of paper printed with the image of a tobacco leaf for the payment of goods and services and the settlement of debts. Various types of commodities (for example grain) were used as "country money" to pay taxes and other obligations to the local colonial authorities in all of the English colonies right up until the advent of the American Revolutionary War (1776-1781). However, in Virginia the tobacco farmers could also make payment in the tobacco currency.

Soon afterwards, an entirely new adventure in the history paper money unfolded in the context of military conflict and radical political change known to us today as the American Revolution. This exciting moment in the evolution of money was based on the young nation's paper currency. These paper bills did the job of paying for armed conflict with the mother

---

[3] Breen, T.H., *Tobacco and Culture: The Mentality of the Great Tidewater Planters on the Eve of Revolution.* Princeton: The University Press, 1985. A picture of a $5dollar tobacco note may be found on p.42.

country, but later gave rise to the pejorative expression, "Not worth a Continental." Like the French and the Russian revolutions to follow, the American Revolution was achieved with the assistance of an unsecured paper currency. What followed, of course, was that the young nation suffered the inflation that paper money often creates. To say how and why this happened, however, would be to rush ahead of our story.

After the many forms of commodity money described earlier had evolved so as to permit regular market activity in societies around the world, the evolution of money went on to include a phase in which the precious and semi-precious metals gold, silver, and copper were substituted for other, less convenient, commodities. The metals that were chosen to play role of stars in the firmament of many other types of commodity money all possessed the following three essential qualities:

- **portability** (a gold or silver coin is more easily carried than an ox or a bushel of barley)
- **durability** (gold is almost entirely chemically inert and silver a little less so)
- **divisibility** (gold and silver are relatively divisible but oxen, and deerskins are not).

Although coins of silver or gold might show some wear and tear after years of being passed from hand to hand (and "sweated", "clipped" or otherwise debased), a gold or silver ingot or coin was, obviously, not subject to the same kind of friction with the environment as was Virginia's tobacco

22

currency. In short, gold and silver coins were relatively durable, could be made in smaller and smaller denominations, and were much more portable than most other forms of commodity money. The more valuable coins that were deliberately retired from circulation by their owners did not even have to be particularly "durable." Thus, the savvy merchant and the wealthy landowner tended to keep the "better" (i.e., not "clipped" or debased) coins they received in trade to amass as savings. Please welcome what is perhaps the best known principle of monetary economics known as "Gresham's Law!"

Briefly, Sir Thomas Gresham (1519-1597), simply pointed out that the coins that had not been subjected to "clipping", "sweating", or debasement by the monarch would be usually be withdrawn from circulation because of their relatively higher precious metal content. This natural response of most people towards their money would leave only the battered or debased coins in circulation. While the same effect had been noticed by Aristophanes (in his 5th Century BC play called "The Frogs"), and by no less a theorist than Copernicus (1473-1543), we still tend to state Gresham's Law much as Gresham himself did by saying that: "Bad money drives out good."

Gresham's Law, however, also covers a much bigger problem than the problem presented by the clipping and debasing of coins to remove some of their precious metal content. Gresham's insight is also useful for understanding the problems that arise when both gold and silver are used as currency. When this happens the monetary problems associated with what was called "bi-metallism" raise their ugly heads. This unhappy state of affairs was noted most trenchantly by Sir Isaac Newton (1643 -1727) in his role as the Master of the Royal Mint. No less than two centuries after Newton's day, the same "bi-metallism problem" also provided the monetary backdrop for the great American orator William Jennings Bryan's most famous oracular pronouncement : "Thou shall not press down upon labor this crown of thorns. Thou shall not crucify mankind on a cross of gold!"

Leaving the great populist orator's unheeded cry for mercy to a later chapter, it must only be noted here that gold, silver, and copper, were commodity monies that had the quality of being almost infinitely divisible. In other words, what we might call "small change" today could be created in metallic commodity monies by the simple device of making smaller and smaller coins that would facilitate the buying and selling of items both large and small. In fact, most peoples who developed any type of market society at all usually also developed some form of "small change" to make their daily purchases.

Sometimes greedy individuals who had acquired some form of commodity money new to them could be fooled by what they had obtained in trade. The Spanish *conquistador* Bernal Diaz Del Castillo, was, on one occasion, delighted to return home to Cuba with numerous tiny ax heads which he believed to be made of gold. Diaz imagined that he had bargained shrewdly for these charming little trinkets, since he had only offered the grateful natives a handful of green glass beads in exchange. On this occasion, however, the last laugh was on Diaz, for, during the obligatory inspection of the spoils by the Governor of Cuba, it was revealed that what Diaz had acquired in trade was, indeed "small change." The small copper ax heads that Diaz had received in exchange for a handful of green glass beads were, in fact, a form of currency used by the inhabitants of Montezuma's empire.[4]

From Metal to Paper

However, even the gold and silver coins of old were soon left behind when the magic spirit of money changed its nature from that of useful, beautiful, or nutritious commodities to continue as mere slips of paper. This giant step in the development of money happened very early in history with the assistance of, among others, the medieval order of the Knights Templar.[5] These fierce fighters for Christendom not only sallied forth to the Holy Land to retrieve Jerusalem for the true cross, but also operated the first inter-regional banking system to grow up in Europe during the Middle ages. It was only when the good looking but terribly cruel French monarch Phillip IV,

---

[4] Diaz del Castillo, Bernal, *The Conquest of New Spain.* Many editions.
[5] Haag, Michael, *The Templars: The History and the Myth.* New York: Harper, 2009. pp.137-145.

known as "*Philippe le Bel*", destroyed the Knights Templar by means of generous application of torture followed by burning at the stake, that the Templars were replaced as Europe's bankers by the Florentine banking houses of the Medicis, the Guelphs, and the Ghibillines. These family banking operations grew up in Italy during the century following March 18, 1314 when the Grand Master of the Templars, James de Molay, was burned to death on an island in the middle of the Seine with the whole population of Paris looking on.[6]

After that, the powerful banking families of 14th and 15th Century Florence not only patronized artists like Michelangelo and Botticelli, but also quickly replaced the banking networks of the Templars to make their brilliant and beautiful Tuscan city one of the most powerful banking centers of Europe. Before continuing the description of the trials and triumphs of the first examples of European paper money, however, there are one or two problems that plagued the evolution of commodity money that should be briefly noted.

One of the first points often made in discussions concerning the evolution of money that are usually found at the beginning of books on monetary history concerns the perceived shortcomings of barter as a form of economic exchange. Recent work by anthropologists and archeologists, however, may cause us to wonder if barter ever actually existed except, possibly, in

---

[6] Ibid., 237.

moments of tremendous social upheaval such as those occasioned by war, revolution, famine, and natural disasters.

Barter: Did it Ever really Exist?

Barter is often said to have been the basic system of economic exchange that most probably existed in the far simpler human communities of early times. According to the anthropologist Marcell Mauss, however, evidence to support the idea that any society actually functioned on the basis of barter is minimal to non-existent.[7] According to the usual explanation, barter might be employed to facilitate the transaction when, for example, the parents of the groom were required to purchase the young man's bride using a certain number of horses, cows, or goats. This might have worked for a once-in-a-lifetime purchase such as the purchase of a bride, but what about those regularly imagined cases in which the village shoemaker wanted to exchange the products of his labor for a basket of apples only to find that none of the farmers he knows happened to need a pair of sandals? This lack of complementary purchasing desires presents problems, of course, especially in textbooks of elementary economics. There is now, however, considerable doubt that such a system was ever used except in severe emergencies or as a means of settling accounts between enemies, as in the exchange of prisoners for example.

_____

[7] Mauss, Marcel, *The Gift: The Form and Reason for Exchange in Archaic Societies*. New York: Norton, 1967, pp. 36-37.

Even if such a system ever actually functioned in practice, however, the economic shortcoming of simple barter would be that something of much greater value might be traded for something worth much less. Homer, whose great epic poem *The Iliad* was quoted earlier, pictured just such a thing happening once on the great plain of *Ilium* before the walls of Troy. It is entirely possible, of course, that the great Homer was merely indulging in a bit of anti-Trojan irony when he wrote the lines that will be quoted here. It all started in the middle of a long day of battle before the walls of Troy. The unconquerable Diomedes, having killed large numbers of Trojan warriors, spotted the wealthy young Glaucus, a Trojan warrior who had once been Diomedes' "guest friend." The fierce Diomedes decided on the spot to spare Glaucus' life. As a symbol of their friendship, the two fighters then decided to trade their armor:

> *Both agreed. Both fighters sprang from their chariots ,clasped each other's hands and traded pacts of friendship.*
>
> *But the son of Chronus, Zeus, stole Glaucus' wits away. He traded his gold armor for bronze with Diomedes, The worth of a hundred oxen just for nine.*[8]

The great bard Homer was here making his own sly comment on the concept of barter some six or seven centuries before the

---

[8] Fagles, *The Iliad*, p.203.

beginning of the present era. In the somewhat sarcastic lines quoted here, Homer slyly lets us know that, even in that far off Heroic Age, the Greeks knew how to evaluate an exchange of goods in commodity money terms.

It is, of course, amusing to portray situations as the one experienced by Glaucus, or the paradox of the unhappy shoemaker yearning for the taste of apples, as they may have existed in an imaginary village or on a battlefield of the distant past. It is much more likely, however, that our ancestors were a bit more practical than the typical monetary historian has given them credit for. It is much more likely that, even in the most ancient times, a desired trade of qualitatively different items would be conducted with the assistance of some monetary intermediary, in other words with some form of commodity money. In this way, producers of all kinds could enjoy an attractive choice. They could choose to use their surplus commodity money to exchange for other things they wanted to possess, or, alternatively, to amass quantities of their money as a store of wealth that would provide them with future power and security.

Most communities studied by archeologists and anthropologists today show evidence of the use of some sort of commodity used as a monetary intermediary. The list of commodity monies includes: barley (in ancient Babylon); rice (still in use in many communities today); copper ax heads (which, as used in ancient China, provided the origin of the modern word "cash"); and, many other items of daily use both mundane and marvelous. In his very interesting and etymologically rich *The History of Money*, the anthropologist Jack Weatherford points to a number of studies of economic practices in Mexico dating to Aztec times (1248-1521 CE). The authors that Weatherford cites shows how the omnipresent and very useful cocoa bean that grew in tropical Mexico was used to round off the difference in trades where the indivisibility of some desired item made it necessary to throw in a few cocoa beans to close the deal.[9]

There is a profusion of examples of intermediary goods used in this way in the many societies known both to economic historians and to anthropologists. Both types of specialist find numerous examples of such goods used as commodity money today by peoples all around the world. Jack Weatherford's list of useful commodities that have served as money includes: salt (from which our word "salary" is derived); logs (used in Honduras) dried fish (from the Baltic); oxen (as noted in the works of Homer); cattle (the Latin root, *pecunarius*, gives us the modern word "pecuniary"); chattels of all kinds including both animals and slave girls; cigarettes (widely used in US prisons to

---

[9] Weatherford, Jack, *The History of Money*. New York: Crown, 1997. pp.22-27. Visitors to the British Museum may also have seen a display featuring a gold cowry shell. This gold artifact was undoubtedly equal to many natural shells. In the same way, the Aztec practice of filling a cocoa bean husk with gold would have produced a 'golden bean' to equal a large number of the natural kind.

this day); deer skins (giving us our modern expression "The buck stops here."); and finally cowry shells. Why cowry shells?

Why indeed? In the year 1940 professor M.W.D Jeffreys begged to differ with a colleague who had asserted most definitely that the cowry shell did not, in fact, represent the human vulva, but represented, rather, the human eye.[10] The whole point of the cowry shell, Professor Jeffrey's interlocutor thought, was to protect those who wore cowry shells against the evil eye. Professor Jeffreys then brought forward a number of examples which he felt showed clearly that the cowry did, indeed, provide a symbolic representation of the human female *labia majora*. The "Why Indeed?" question here was answered by Professor Jeffries himself who cited extensive evidence to the effect that the supposed utility of this widely encountered commodity money was to insure the fertility of the female.

Meanwhile, a myth told by the Benin people of West Africa tells us how "the king brought cowry money" to the people.[11] The king, in this mythical horror story, took some of his subjects, broke their legs, and put them in a house on a banana plantation. The King's idea here was to feed his newly created cripples on bananas until they grew fat. After these unfortunates grew both large and delicious, they were thrown into the sea. Then, when the cowries began to eat the obese

---

[10] Jeffreys, M.W.D, "Cowry, Vulva, Eye", *Man*, Vol.42, (Sep.-Oct., 1942), p.120.
[7] Gregory, C.A., "Cowries and Conquest: Towards a Subalternate Quality Theory of Money", *Comparative Studies in Society and History*, Vol. 38, No.2. (April, 1966), PP.195-217.

former subjects of the King, their corpses were pulled in. The cowries were then stripped off the dead bodies put in hot water and killed. After this, according to the myth, the cowry shells were used as a type of money called "white corn money"; so as to distinguish cowry shells from other types of commodity money already in use in Benin communities. Before the king of Benin had acted with such resolution and address, his subjects had been required to take dried beans to market if they wanted to buy sweet potatoes for the family larder.

For our purposes, however, it will not be necessary to decide exactly which part of the human body the cowry shell was intended to represent. It will be sufficient merely to say that whatever it was supposed to resemble, cowry shell money has been unearthed from sites found all over the world from what is now Ontario in Canada, to West Africa, and from there all the way to Yunnan in Southwest China. Perhaps Professor Jeffries' guess about the cowry as a fertility charm was correct, but deciding exactly why this interesting looking shell was so widely used as a commodity money is immaterial to our purpose here. The fact that archeologists and anthropologists have found caches of cowry shells tucked away almost everywhere on earth is not.

In fact, the Benin myth about how "the king brought cowries to the people" may indicate something quite interesting about commodity money that might be worth considering before going further. What the Benin myth tells us is that it took quite a lot of human effort to come up with a few portly corpses covered with hungry cowries. This observation will eventually return our discussion when we take up the labor theory of value as part of our discussion of gold mining techniques in Chapter 5. However a brief word on the topic and an introduction one of the first creators of the theory will be useful here.

Adam Smith, as many readers will already know, used the labor theory of value to resolve a paradox that he had imagined for the readers of his famous *The Wealth of Nations* (1776). The argument concerning Smith's use of the labor theory of value will be given in greater detail in Chapter 5, but what may surprise many people is that Adam Smith most probably inherited the labor theory of value from an American subject of the British crown, Benjamin Franklin, who was, beyond any reasonable doubt, one of the most intellectual and scientifically minded personalities among the founders of the Republic. Before going into Ben Franklin's story in more detail, however, it will convenient first to consider the history of historical coinage systems to see what happens to commodity money when the power of the state becomes involved- as it always does.

The Uses of Coinage and the Temptation of the Prince

To restate the functions of money as explained earlier, it should be repeated at this point that money is:

- A medium of exchange (provides payment for goods)

- A unit of account (evaluates all goods and services in terms of a common unit of measure)
- A store of value (preserves earnings permitting the accumulation of wealth).

All of these functions can be gravely compromised when the inherent values of gold or silver commodity money are tampered with by various economic actors, all of whom tend to have the same end in mind -namely to get something for nothing. Briefly, a very long line is formed by those who made a habit of subtracting the precious metals (gold and silver) from the coinage so as to enjoy a bit of unearned income for themselves. The line begins with the coin clipper and counterfeiter, and extends all the way up through the social hierarchy to the Prince of the Realm.

Compared to cocoa beans or tobacco, the superior qualities (portability, durability, and divisibility) of the precious metals could have permitted a stable and reliable pattern of economic exchange to take place in the markets of the past- had it not been for two rather difficult problems. The first problem had to do with the amount of precious metals that the monarch allowed to remain in gold and silver coins after gold and silver had become the basis of a coinage. The second problem had to do with the instability of the relative values of those two metals.[12] The constantly changing relative values of gold and

---

[12] A notable exception here would be the Swedish "coins" of the early modern period which were large copper ingots weighing several pounds.

silver, for example, were expressed in what was called an "exchange ratio." The exchange ratio expressed the relative values of the gold and silver used to create any particular coinage. In ancient Rome, for example, the exchange ratio was set at 25 (silver) to 1 (golden) coin. The Roman ratio reflected the fact that there was much less gold than silver available in the Mediterranean societies of Classical times. After the Spaniards' discovery of both silver and gold in the Americas, however, the silver: gold ratio was much more often 16 : 1.

The variable relation between gold and silver changed through time, however, as the amount of gold and silver available from mining activities changed. When, for example, massive gold supplies were discovered in mid-19th Century California, the exchange ratio observed in the United States experienced constant change. This, as we will see later on, created a century long war between those Americans who loved silver and those who preferred gold as the principal monetary metal. Throughout history, however, the variability of the silver/gold ratio led to the persistence of the "bi-metallism problem." This problem challenged all sorts of interesting characters in history from Isaac Newton, Master of the Royal Mint, to William Jennings Bryan, the "boy orator of the Platte."

The gold and silver used in trade had not always been as reliably pure in quality as they had finally become either in Isaac Newton's or William Jennings Bryan's lifetime. It was usually the case that gold used as a medium of exchange in the early days of market society was not exactly of the 99.99 or "24 karat" level of purity. On the contrary, the gold coins or bars brought to market from one part of the world may not have been as pure (and hence as valuable) as gold bars brought from some other location. This could have been the case for natural reasons, since gold can occur mixed with another substances as in the case of a hybrid precious metal called "Electrum", an alloy of gold and silver.

For all of its mixed quality, however, Electrum was the substance used in some of the first coins ever issued as we shall see momentarily. The relative purity/impurity of gold and silver, however, may also have been the result of simple human lust for that sort gain that may be achieved without actually working. Gold can be readily mixed with other cheaper metals such as copper- a fact that excited the cupidity of many dealers in precious metals and metal currencies known to history. When gold was debased by the addition of less valuable metals, this necessarily affected its' exchange value.   The money changers of ancient markets, therefore, had a simple procedure to provide themselves with a rough estimate of the purity of precious metals offered in exchange. This procedure involved a piece of stone against which precious metals could be rubbed to estimate their relative purity. Our modern word "touchstone" comes from the relatively unsophisticated practice of rubbing pieces of gold or silver against an abrasive piece of stone. The purer metal, being softer, will leave a larger mark on the "touchstone", and will be accepted as more, rather than less, valuable. The variable purity of bars or ingots of precious metal offered in trade presented a problem, of course, but a much bigger problem arrived with another important step in the evolution of money, namely, the invention of coinage.

Now we may return to a problem noted earlier. This is the problem created by the greed of rulers which we may call "the temptation of the Prince." The invention of coinage usually required the existence of some political authority, a king for example, who was able to "guarantee" that the coins stamped with his name and adorned with image were comprised of a given weight and purity of precious metal. When the first coins appeared, therefore, it suddenly became possible to conclude a market transaction by the simple device of counting the coins needed to complete the sale. The alternative was purchase by weight of precious metal, that is, by going to the scales which were themselves always an object of suspicion. It is likely, therefore, that the volume of market transactions leaped skyward with the invention of the coinage of precious and semi-precious metals. The reason, of course, was that accepting payment by tale (i.e., by counting) instead of by weight was so much more convenient. There was also, however, a dark side to this development.

The first coins that we know about may have been minted in the Anatolian kingdom of Lydia which took up a large part of what is now Turkey. The Lydian king Croesus (595-547

BCE) is often said to have introduced the first coins ever created which made of "electrum." In fact, it may have been Croesus' predecessor, King Alyattes, who actually launched the coinage in the late 6th or early 5th Century BC. Nor is it entirely clear that the Lydian was really a coin. Since the Lydian contains neither inscription nor the image of the monarch who is said to have issued it, some numismatists believe that the gold disc in question was merely a badge or a medal.

An earlier candidate for the title of first coinage would be the sea turtle coinage struck on the island of Aegina (near Athens) as early as the 8th Century BCE. The turtle coinage has clearly been identified with the city state that issued it. As was the case with the Athenian *Drachma* issued later on, the image on the Agenitian coin is commonly associated with its place of origin and not with a royal or political ruler.

This was necessary, of course, since, in both the Agenitian and Athenian cases, the authority issuing the coinage was a democratic city state which, obviously, lacked a monarch looking sternly towards the horizon on the face of its coins. The Athenian *Drachma* is, by the way, unusual among the examples of coinage in the ancient world, because during the two centuries or so during which it was the dominant currency of the Aegean region, it was never debased.

One good reason for the never diminished purity of the Athenian *Drachma* was the fact that the Athenians possessed their own silver mine at Lauium in eastern Attica. There, the silver produced by slave labor flowed freely into the counting

A Lydian 1/3 Stater [13]

houses of rich Athenians who sent their slaves to work in the mine. The amounts of silver mined at Laurium increased noticeably after a new and very rich vein of silver was discovered just after the first Persian invasion of Greece headed by the Persian Emperor Darius (550-486 BCE). The silver from Laurium flowed even more freely than before, right down to the second invasion of Greece headed by Darius' son Xerxes (485-4465 BCE).[14] The first invasion, led by Darius, had failed because the Persians had chosen the narrow beach of Marathon in Eastern Attica to land their vast invasion force where they were decisively defeated by Athenian hoplites waiting for them

---

[13] Imaged sourced at: http://en.wikipedia.org/wiki/Coin

[14] Herodotus, *The Histories*. Books VI-VII.

in what still ranks as one of the biggest military upsets in history.

The Athenian *Drachma*: Known as "the Owl"[15]

The second Persian invasion of Greece headed by Darius' son Xerxes also failed, however, and this failure was in no small part the direct result of the economic power of Athenian silver. Right after the defeat of the Persians at Marathon, an Athenian politician, Themistocles, talked his fellow citizens into using the wealth created by a recent silver strike at Laurium to build the Athenian navy. This done, Themistocles used his new navy very intelligently to defeat a much larger force of Persians and their allies in the naval battle that took place in the straights of Salamis. An angry and disappointed Xerxes watched the whole thing from his portable throne set on a cliff high above the action, and decided that, even though he had already burnt the city of Athens to the ground, it was time to leave the Greeks alone.[16]

---

[15] Image sourced at: http://www.wisdomportal.com/Haikus/OwlGreekCoin.jpg
[16] Herodotus, Book VIII: 70-97.

Most political authorities mentioned in the history of the coinage, however, were not as honorable as the Athenians had been concerning the weight and purity of the *Drachma*. The dark side of the history of coinage was provided by later greedy and improvident kings and dictators who, throughout the history of coinage, have responded to either their governmental or personal lack of funds by the "debasement" of their coinage. Debasement was accomplished by the royal leader in the following three steps: 1) recalling the coinage; 2) melting the coins; and, 3) issuing a new coinage containing less precious metal than before while leaving in place the same inscriptions and "guarantees" that the coin had previously borne. The precious metal content of the coins removed in this way was, of course, destined for the royal or imperial treasury- if not for the private strongboxes of the ruler in question. Once marooned in the monarch's private hoard, the monetary truism referred to earlier as "Gresham's Law" kept it there. Probably the worst debasers of the coin of the realm known to history were the Roman emperors.

Many rulers throughout history have taxed (or robbed from) their subjects by means of the debasement of the currency. The Roman Empire, however, provides the most flagrant example of this form of securing the finances of the state. The gold coin of the Romans, the *aureus*, was not widely used, either the days of the Roman Republic, or in the days of the Roman Empire that followed. The Roman Republic came to an end when Caesar's nephew Gaius Octavius, later called "Augustus" (63 BCE - 14 CE), emerged as the victor in the civil war that followed Julius Caesar's death at the hands of Brutus and his fellow knife-wielding senators.

As mentioned earlier, the Romans estimated the relative ratio of silver to gold at 25 to 1. In other words, twenty-five silver *Denarius* were required to purchase one *Aureus*. The Romans, of course, did not at first have their own mines of precious metals. They were, therefore, required to remove the gold they needed from the safekeeping of their neighbors after having attacked their cities and razed them to the ground. One such unfortunate neighbor of the Romans was the city of Carthage which yielded not only the wealth behind its walls, but also rich mines of gold and silver in what is now Spain.

After that, it was Gresham's law that was responsible for keeping the golden *aureus* locked in the strongboxes of the wealthy Romans. This was because, silver being much more available, it became the "bad money" that drove out the "good." Thus, the Romans relied on the lesser coins of silver, copper, and brass to do the daily work of the market place. The gold *Aureus*, therefore, remained the relatively more valuable coin of the Roman realm which, of course, became more and more valuable with each imperial debasement that occurred. This began with the Roman emperor Nero's (37-68 CE) first debasement of the Roman *Denarius*. It was, then, the silver *Denarius* rather than the *aureus*, that would suffer the hammer blows of continual debasement ordered by later Roman emperors.

After Nero, then, the Emperor Trajan (98 to 117 CE) cut the silver content of the *Denarius* down to 85 percent of its former silver content. Trajan was the emperor who extended the Roman Empire to its maximum territorial point, and who discovered, as have later empire builders, that it takes a lot of money to keep an empire going. Finally, the philosophical Emperor Marcus Aurelius (161-180 CE) cut a further 10% of the silver content out of the long suffering *Denarius*. These regular debasements continued throughout the reigns of successive Emperors most of whom debased the silver currency of the Romans so that, by the 3rd Century of the Common Era, the Roman "silver" coin was only 5% silver by weight.[17]

Because of the relatively small amounts of gold held by the successive Roman emperors, the twin realities of bi-metallism and Gresham's Law were not included in the many difficulties with which the later Roman emperors had to contend. Some thirteen centuries later on, however, Sir Isaac Newton in England found that he had a very interesting problem on his hands arising from the bi-metallism of the English currency in his day. Newton's problem was one that would continue to trouble monetary authorities and the body politic at large from the early years of the 18th Century right down to the

---

[17] Jones, A.H.M., "Inflation Under the Roman Empire", *The Economic History Review*, Vol.5, No.3. pp.293-318.

day on which William Jennings Bryan pronounced his immortal "cross of gold" oration. The problem was caused by using two precious metals in the management of a national currency.

Sir Isaac Newton's "Cross of Gold"

After sorting out the motion of the celestial spheres, Newton became the Master of the Royal Mint in London. In this position, Newton had first to deal with two major problems. The first was the public crime of counterfeiting, and the second was the monetary nuisance created by a bi-metallic currency. The first problem Newton solved relatively easily. He simply had several prominent counterfeiters captured and hung by the neck until dead much to the joy of the populace and the comfort of the commercial community. The second problem with which the sage of the solar system and the inventor of the calculus had to deal was a bit more difficult to address. This was a problem which arose from the fact that the English coinage of Newton's day consisted both of silver and of gold.

The problems caused by the bi-metallic standard used in Great Britain in those days were created when the conditions of production in each of those metals caused their relative values to vary. When the market value of silver rose above the value stated on the face of the coins, the well to do subjects of the King were either too slow or entirely unwilling to bring their silver to the Mint to be stamped out as new coins. This was simply because the market savvy Englishman of those days knew that he could get a better price for his silver almost anywhere other than at the Royal Mint. Newton took up the problem by addressing himself to " *To the Rt. Honble. the Lords Commrs. ol his Mats Treary."* as follows:

Gold is therefore in Spain & Portugal of sixteen times more value than silver of equal weight & allay, according to the standard of those Kingdoms. At which rate a Guinea is worth 22s. 1 d. But this high price keeps their gold at home in good plenty, & carries away the Spanish Silver into all Europe, so that at home they make their payments in Gold, & will not pay in Silver without a premium.[18]

As the man in charge of keeping the amount of silver coins required for trade both numerous and heavy, Newton felt disadvantaged when market price for silver rose higher than the official price offered at the Mint. The reason being that it was this caused merchants and others who had to settle overseas debt to send their silver coins out of the country where they would be valued at a premium rather than at the official prices offered by the Royal Mint. One result of such imbalance was that the savvy money changers who followed what today we would call the "forex" (or the foreign exchange) market melted down the silver coins originally issued by the Royal Mint and sold the

---

[18] Newton's report to the Masters of the Treasury is entitled "Sir Isaac Newton's Report of the State of Gold and Silver Coin" and is dated 25 September 1717. Available online at:
http://www.pierre-marteau.com/editions/1701-25-mint-reports/report-1717-09-25.htmli

silver thus produced as ingots. These, of course, received prices in excess of the official value of the silver coins originally brought to the Mint for re-coinage. Newton expressed the problem that this created as follows:

> It is the demand for exportation which hath raised the price of exportable Silver about 2d. or 3d. in the ounce above that of Silver in coyn, and have thereby created a temptation to export or melt down the silver coyn rather then give 2d. or 3d. for forreign silver.[19]

Newton closed his report to "Yor Lordps." by pointing out that it was always possible that their was enough "plate" (i.e., silver) in the kingdom to reduce the value of silver relative to that of gold. However, Newton pointed out, it was equally possible that gold might also flow into Great Britain. This would lower the relative value of gold, and thereby bring the market value of silver back up to the official price established at the Royal Mint.

Indeed, as later research has shown, gold did slowly decline in value relative to silver and the great exodus of silver from Great Britain that Newton was worried about never took place.[20] Nevertheless, the markets of Great Britain and

---

[19] Ibid.
[20] Van der Wee, Herman, "Money, Credit, and Banking Systems", The Cambridge Economic History of Europe. London: Cambridge University Press, 1977, p.297.

continental Europe continued to be affected by the differences between nominal value of any given national coinage and the real value of its metallic content for many years after Newton wrote. It was only after the next milestone in the evolution of money had been passed, namely the general acceptance of paper "promises to pay", that the shortcomings of a system of payment based on gold and silver coins could become past history.

What this brief historical review has demonstrated is that even while there were several kinds of problems associated with gold and silver as the dominant commodity monies, that the role of precious metals in the evolution of money has been a constant one. With this thought in mind it is now time to consider this problem in modern terms and in a completely practical way, by advancing an answer to your first question which is: "Why should I buy gold?"

Chapter 2   Why Should I Buy Gold?

We can begin with a very short answer to the question, "Why should I buy gold?" When certain unstable economic conditions develop you should buy gold for one very simple reason- because it is money. This is the easy part. The more difficult questions arise around the historical process by which gold became money. In the brief explanation that follows here it will become clear that gold became the emperor of the metals used as money down through history because it embodied the necessary qualities of a commodity money in the most complete way.

To begin with gold has the longest history as a metal used and hoarded by people down through the ages. This is true because gold was one of the first metals to be found in nature in a relatively pure form. For this reason gold was also one of the first metals to be worked by human beings. Gold was transformed into useful and beautiful objects in the absence of metallurgical techniques developed later in history. Gold, therefore, has been treasured by all manner of peoples down through time. From the wandering Scythian steppe dwellers of Herodotus' day, down through the bankers of the late Medieval Italian city states, and on to the present government of the United States which keeps no less than 8,000 tons of gold in its secure storage facility at Fort Knox, Kentucky. In a note to *The Financial Times*, Harvard professor Jonathon Zittrain pointed out that the US government maintains a defense force for Fort Knox that includes gun ships, tanks, and 30,000 soldiers. It appears, then, that even if the Government of United States does not hold this fortune in gold as a reserve against financial claims, someone in government still believes that the possession of gold is an important safeguard against emergencies. It is most probable that the American gold hoard is meant to be used as emergency money in case of war, famine, or natural disaster, if and when other systems of payment may have broken down.

Given examples of this nature, it will be quite easy to understand why it is that gold has played a key role in human economic society since very early times and why it continues to retain its' monetary role today. The answer to the question "Why should I buy gold?", therefore, is directly related both to the three essential qualities of a successful commodity money, and to the three basic functions of money. Gold, as we shall see, is the emperor of the commodity monies for the simple reason that the three essential qualities of gold allow it to fulfill the three functions of money most effectively.

The Three Qualities of Successful Commodity Money

The physical characteristics that make for a successful commodity money were mentioned earlier. They are: 1) portability; 2) divisibility; and, 3) durability. The **portability** of gold, when combined with its very high value-to-weight ratio, made the shiny yellow metal very convenient for carrying out the first function of money which is that of a medium of exchange.

Similarly, the physical characteristics of gold- its highly malleable nature and consequent easy **divisibility** -allowed gold coins of all sizes to be produced in the various coinage systems that were developed in the market histories of many societies. Conversely, many of the other forms of commodity money discussed in the previous chapter were not readily divisible at all. For example, consider the form of commodity money mentioned in Homer's *Iliad*, namely oxen. One hundred of these large slow beasts would have been required to buy the Trojan hero Glaucus' golden armor as Homer told the story, but one hundred and a half oxen would not have been a feasible price. Oxen are divisible, of course, but only if you want to use one as the main course for a giant Texas barbeque and not as a means of payment. In a more timely example diamonds, which many people still like to collect, are not really "divisible" at all and, accordingly, have not played a role in monetary systems.

It is perhaps in its quality of **durability** that gold most completely out performs all other forms of commodity money. Because of gold's inherent physical characteristic which is that it is almost completely chemically inert, it is more durable than the other precious and semi-precious metals used in the past as commodity money. Gold is also much more durable than other forms of commodity money discussed earlier, for example, tobacco, cocoa beans, and *shekels* of barley. Keeping both the functions and qualities of a successful commodity money in mind, will make it easier to understand some of the following answers to the question: "Why should I buy gold?"

The Three Functions of Money

Gold has played a key role in monetary systems for a very long time. For many millennia, gold has been the commodity that could be used to buy other commodities including both the necessities and the luxuries of life. In short, gold's long history as a commodity valued and cherished throughout human history has made it a universal means of payment that may be used anywhere and any time as a **medium of exchange**.

Because gold filled the medium of exchange function so universally and so well, it could also very be very conveniently used to price all other commodities once any given society had reached that stage of development wherein marketing plays a large part in every day life. This is why, in some accounts, gold has been baptized as a "universal commodity." Very early in human economic history, therefore, gold was a widely used and entirely reliable **"unit of account."** Any thing that someone in a marketplace anywhere in the world and at most any time in human history could always be priced in gold.

Finally, due to its physical characteristic of being almost completely chemically inert, chemical gold has served throughout history as a very reliable **"store of value."** This characteristic allowed both the hard working and the merely fortunate to accumulate wealth and to preserve it effectively.

It was perhaps this clearly superior quality of gold that caused it to be so relied upon through the many epochs of economic instability, war and social disruption that have characterized human history. Nevertheless, gold is still a very paradoxical commodity. Why, for example, do gold miners remove it from deep in the earth in, for example South Africa so that bankers can to place it once again in their vaults also located deep below the surface of the earth?

While there may be no easy or obvious logic that will help us to unravel this paradox, the following chapters will show that the role that gold has played in human history has been a crucial one. In earlier times gold allowed ambitious rulers to make war and to conquer territories. In our own day, when economies fail, international trade slows down, and war clouds loom on the horizon, people all around the world still move to preserve their wealth by holding gold. This is the lesson of history. It is also, however, the answer to the question that serves as the title of this brief chapter. The reason that you may come to decide to buy gold in one of the many ways in which it is now possible to do this is as follows. If you are concerned about the future will buy gold for two reasons: 1) because gold is money; and, 2) also because gold is one of the few kinds of money that will retains its value- even through very difficult times.

Janus Sees Both the Future and the Past[21]

Janus Looks Ahead But What Does He See?

The development of money through human history may remind us of the god Janus, the Roman deity after whom the first month of the year is named. Janus has two faces. One looks forward into the future, and one looks backwards towards the past. Where the development of money in the past is concerned,

---

[21] Image sourced at: http://www.probertencyclopaedia.com/j/Janus.jpg

Janus looks back over five thousand years during which time human communities used various forms of commodity money to buy and sell things. Since then, of course, paper money has come to dominate human commercial and financial affairs. The expression "paper money" is used for convenience here, since it is a phrase that covers several different types of monetary innovation. In fact, the proportion of "paper money" that is actually on paper is, today, quite low. It makes up about three to almost ten percent of all money as compared to what we could call "digital money." Digital money is the kind of money in your bank account and expended through the medium of your checkbook. Percentages of "cash" that are in metallic currency (no longer containing precious metal) in all likelihood, represent a very small proportion of all money.

Thus, while Janus may have already looked into the future well beyond digital money, we cannot yet imagine what he may have seen. Unlike ourselves, however, Janus may be able to look into the future to see a world in which financial markets are, once again, in an uproar. He might also be able to view a scene in which, once again, national governments are called in to save the bankers from their fantasies and their follies.[22] Janus might even be able to observe the chaos that might someday

---

[22] "Fantasies" may be a kind word in this context. For a sharper verdict on the activities of bankers, hedge fund managers, and other speculators see Phillips, Kevin, *Bad Money: Reckless Finance, Failed Politics, and the Global Crisis of American Capitalism*. Revised Edition, New York: Penguin, 2009. Especially the *"Preface"*, pp. xl-lxxiv.

occur when the financial maneuvers of bankers, speculators, and politicians have made, still another, mess of things. At worst, what Janus may be viewing as he looks into the future is the mass public hysteria that always accompanies a runaway inflation.

What Kind of Money Do We Have Today?

Situated in time somewhere between the commodity monies of the past and the so-called "fiat money" that we all must use today, there were many long periods when "representative money" was the standard. Representative money was used: to meet the needs of commerce; to provide an international standard of value; and, to be treasured as a reliable store of wealth. The word "*fiat*" is the imperative form of the Latin verb *facio* meaning "to do" or "to perform." Thus the word "fiat" could be somewhat colloquially translated as: "Just do it!" In more formal English, when something is done by "fiat" it is done in response to an authoritative command by the government. What really makes "fiat money" different from the other types of money that preceded it, however, is the fact that unlike "representative money", for example, "fiat money" cannot be redeemed at the bank for an equivalent amount of gold or silver.

There were several periods in past history during which "representative money" was widely used. From the moment of its foundation in 1694, the Bank of England for example, issued paper notes "representing" the Pound Sterling (originally a pound of silver) for many years. The use of paper "promises to pay", no doubt, facilitated both the conduct of commerce and economic development not only in Great Britain itself, but also in what was soon to become the British Empire. The best known period in which representative money powered international trade was that of the 19th Century gold standard which drove both the industrial revolutions and the empire building of the Western European countries.

During that brief period, what is now called "representative money" consisted of letters and numbers printed on a piece of paper. The piece of paper "promised to pay" the bearer a certain amount of physical money (usually gold or silver) on demand. Such notes could (most of the time) actually be handed in at the bank in exchange for gold and/or silver coin.[23] The fact that the so-called "banknotes" were, most often, not handed into the bank in exchange for "specie" (i.e., for precious metal) stands as a tribute to one of the most important aspects of a successful monetary system. This was the willingness of the financial sector, of the commercial public, and of the ordinary citizen to believe that there was always enough gold and silver in the bank to satisfy their claims should they suddenly wish to give up the convenience of paper, and go back

---

[23] This requirement was sometimes lifted in time of war, eg, in Great Britain during WW1.

to carrying gold and silver coins in a strong leather pouch attached to a heavy belt around their waist.

It was, indeed, only the willingness of both the businessman and the ordinary citizen to trust not only the political and monetary authorities of their countries but also their country's bankers, that made paper money possible in the first place. A piece of paper without such guarantees is, after all, intrinsically worthless. When such trust on the part of those who regularly use money (i.e., almost all of us) disappears, much of the magic quality of money also evaporates into a mist of economic uncertainty. When this happens, what often goes with it is a decline in the level of economic activity and the onset of what working people once called "hard times."

Many such periods in the past began with a "run on the bank." In a much younger America the "run on the bank" was a regular feature of the economic crises that took place with a stunning degree of regularity. These included the "panics" of 1837, 1857, 1873, 1893, and 1907, to mention only the major ones. A "run on the bank" was a disturbing phenomenon that, thankfully, has not been seen much in recent times. Indeed, until the economic upheaval very recently caused by the (2007-2008) meltdown in financial markets, the concept of a "run on the bank" had been banished to the history books. In 2007, however, long lines of people in the United Kingdom, anxiously formed in front of a British bank called (somewhat inappropriately) "Northern Rock." They wanted their money back. Until then, there had not been a "run on the bank" in the UK since 1867.

"Representative money", then, worked reasonably well for the brief period in the later 19th and very early 20th Centuries when an international gold standard was in force.[24] The assumptions and institutions which made the international Gold Standard a temporary success during that period were developed through a very long historical process. This process was marked not only with vigorous periods of economic growth, but also by moments of national and international economic crisis. These moments of crisis were accompanied by failing banks, high levels of unemployment, and the eerie sound of national economies screeching to a halt. During such periods, the bank failures added up to numbers that are hard to believe today. The most careful monetary history of the United States tells us that there were something like 9,000 bank failures in the United States during the Great Depression. The year 1933 alone saw no less than 4,000 of these.[25]

One consequence of this disaster was that the newly elected President, Franklin Delano Roosevelt, asked for, and was granted by Congress, a law that made it illegal for US citizens to hold gold. The immediate benefit of this act was, of course, to

---

[24] A brisk and accessible account of the gold standard prefaced by a description of the David Hume (1711-1776) general equilibrium model explaining how it worked is available in Eichengreen, Barry, *Globalizing Capital: A History of the International Monetary System.* Princeton: University Press, 1996, pp. 25-32.
[25] Friedman, Milton and Schwarz Anna, *A Monetary History of the United States.* Princeton: Princeton University Press, 1963, p.353.

protect what was left of the banking sector. When FDR's monetary innovation was made law, the payment function of gold was restricted to international trade, and the era of "representative money" came to an end within American borders. International trade, on the other hand, continued on the gold standard until President Richard M. Nixon reacted to the economic stresses and strains of the day (1971) by placing the whole world on the "fiat money" system. This was a fascinating development that will be explained further in Chapter 11 which is about gold, money, and oil."[26]

Paper Money and the Banks

As the expression "banking sector" used in the previous section will have suggested, the growth of "representative money" (i.e. pieces of paper that "represented" commodities such as gold and silver) went hand in hand with the evolution of banking down through human history. The following description and analysis of representative money will take us, therefore, back to the misty beginnings of historical time. This means that we will begin, as do the *Torah*, the *Bible*, and the

---

[26] The great economist and author of books on economics for the non-specialist, J. K. Galbraith, describes particularly well the period in which representative money was used to great advantage, but also points to a number of periods wherein "representative money" had to bend its knee in the face of war and revolution. Galbraith, J.K., *Money: Whence it Came and Where it Went.* New York: Houghton-Mifflin, 1975. See especially, pp.136-137.

Koran, in Mesopotamia where- as many still believe -the Garden of Eden was located.

It is conventional to accept the still very legible hand-engraved ceramic tablets of the various Middle Eastern civilizations dating back to two and three millennia BCE as marking the beginning of recorded history. The word "bank", of course, only goes back to the Roman word for "bench", which was where the Roman money changer laid out his wares and did his business. What we can identify as "banking", however, began long before. "Banking", on a very general definition, includes: 1) accepting deposits; 2) making loans; and, 3) issuing "promises" or "orders" to pay.

There, between the Tigris and the Euphrates or along the Nile, the development of riverine agriculture made possible the creation of agricultural surpluses. These surpluses required strong and secure places in which to store the grains that made possible future harvests possible as well to provide the staff of life of those who had grown and harvested them. In Mesopotamia, for example, the basic unit of commodity money was the *shekel* which was the standard measure of barley. Those who guarded the stored grain, usually the priests of the temple, created a money economy and managed to do this without sitting behind a bench covered with piles of coins, as did the Roman "bankers" who followed several millennia later. In ancient Egypt, too, something like banking took place, also in the absence of a coinage system. If we wish to regard the visages of the Pharaohs we must visit their tombs for we shall not find their faces on the coin of the realm.

As in Mesopotamia, the grain in Egypt was stored in secure places. Written orders to the keepers of the grain storehouses to release a given quantity of grain also circulated as paper money- or as "papyrus money" in this case.[27] It will come as no surprise, therefore, that in most histories of banking it is suggested that the very first banking activities may have begun in Mesopotamia and Egypt thousands of years ago. Such activities, most authors say, antedated the invention of money where "money" refers to precious metals exchanged by weight and/or a metallic coinage exchanged by tale. The first "banks", then, were probably religious temples in which the agricultural produce of the surrounding community was stored for safekeeping. If this is true, then it seems to follow that the guardians of such temples, the priests, would have been the first "bankers." If so, it was most probably the priests of the temple who initiated one of the first services of banking; namely, the magical act of turning debt into money.

In the year 1889, a certain Mr. Thomas J. Pinches was sitting in the British Museum studying some recently acquired ceramic tablets that had originated in ancient Babylon. Mr. Pinches then wrote to suggest that another scholar, a Mr. Boscawen, was probably mistaken in asserting that the wealthy

---

[27] Davies, G. *A History of Money from Ancient Times to the Present Day.* Cardiff, Wales: University of Wales Press, 1994.

family of the Egibis once resident in Babylon were "bankers." As Pinches explained in his note, he had previously read many tablets describing: "...buying and selling, and lending money, goods, produce and slaves." Mr. Pinches was, however, unwilling to describe the Egibi family of Babylon as "bankers." Pinches did, however, point out in his essay that: "I have found one isolated case in which one person draws upon another for money due to him, but whether it was a real true banking account is uncertain."[28] While the activities that Mr. Pinches read about on the ceramic tablets he was perusing are precisely those that will be treated as banking in what follows here, he was not convinced that the people who performed them were "true bankers." Perhaps if they had worn top hats...?

By the time that the first "historian", Herodotus of Helicarnassus, was writing, however, the banker's role in ancient societies was well established.[29] This seems to have been true not only in the ancient communities of Mesopotamia, but also in Lydia, a country that was located in what is now Turkey. Lydia was a large and prosperous land which had been an aggressive and independent kingdom until Croesus (the

[28] Pinches, Theordore, G., "Babylonian Banking Houses", *The Old and New Testament*, Vol.9, No.1, (July, 1889), pp. 27-28.
[29] Lateiner, Dponald, Ed., *The Histories*, Herodotus. New York: Barnes and Noble Classics, 2004. Herodotus was writing in the 5th Century BCE and is believed to have given public readings of his work in Athens between 449 and 447 BCE.

monarch mentioned earlier for his association with the first coinage) had been defeated by Darius of Persia.[30]

On his way to lead a Persian invasion of Hellas for the second time Darius' son, Xerxes, met with a wealthy Lydian called "Pythios." Pythios had been so kind as to provide food and drink for Xerxes' army when it had passed through Lydia. Thus, when Pythios met the Persian Emperor for the first time he also felt bold enough to offer Xerxes further financing for the Persians' war against the Greeks. From the description of his wealth, and judging by the nature of his conversation with Xerxes, it seems safe to say that Pythios was a banker. At any rate, the wealthy Lydian confessed to the Persian Emperor that he possessed 2,000 talents of silver and that with only 70,000 more "Daric Staters" of gold his holdings would amount to four million gold coins.[31]

Xerxes offered his thanks for the hospitality that Pythios had shown his troops, and also promised the banker a gift of 70,000 gold Staters so that Pythios could then say that he possessed four million of the same. The Daric Stater, we may note in passing, had been named after Xerxes' father Darius, and this may have been one reason for the Emperor's sudden moment of generosity. It is equally possible, however, that the

---

[30] The title of Herodotus' famous work is *The Histories*, however in the classical Greek in which the book was written, the word "histories" meant "enquiries." Herodotus, *The Histories*. For the story of the Persian banker Pythios see book VII Chapters 26-29 and 38 and 39.

[31] The Babylonian "talent" was a measure of weight equal to about 30 kilograms, while the "Daric Stater" was equal to a little more than a half ounce of gold.

mention by Pythios of his 70,000 Stater shortfall was simply a polite way for Pythios the banker to inform Xerxes the Emperor of the size of the tab run up by His Excellency's army.

What happened afterwards, however, might suggest that Xerxes was somewhat piqued by the fact that Pythios was probably as rich as he was. Thus, when the banker very humbly asked the Emperor to release Pythios' eldest son (the first of five) from the duty of making war upon the Greeks, Xerxes, in a fit of rage, had the unfortunate young man cut in two after which he marched his entire army through the two halves of the corpse which had been placed on either side of the road. Herodotus here offers an early example of the relationships between bankers and princes. The relationships between wealthy bankers and the government, we must hope, have improved considerably in our own times. Certainly nothing that happened during the (2008) failure of New York City's Lehman Brothers Investment Bank, and the subsequent $790 Billion bank bailout affair would cause us to think otherwise, although more recent revelations considering bankers Goldman Sachs who made billions by playing both sides of the game with their clients during the same period could change things.[32] The Securities and Exchange Commission is investigating.

---

[32] Goldman bundled mortgage securities under the name "Hudson Mezzanine", and then shorted the very same instrument via the derivatives market, thus reaping billions of dollars as Goldman customers lost theirs. See: Jonathon Ford and Sam Jones, "A Tricky Pick", *The Financial Times*, June 10, 2010.

Banking in Classical Times

In 5th Century Athens the story of banking leaves the realm of myth and story telling and enters historical time. Athens was not only home to the glorious temple of Athena known as the Parthenon, but also hosted a busy inter-regional commerce and the banking activities that developed to facilitate international trade. By the 5th Century, the population of Athens had long outgrown the capacity of the dry and stony lands of Attica to feed the population. Athens had also acquired an empire, as some later countries would also do in the aftermath of major wars. In Athens' case, empire was created following the second unsuccessful invasion of Greece by the Persians referred to earlier. As mentioned, Xerxes' invasion of Greece was followed by a war in which the Athenians had led the other Greeks to victory with the aid of the powerful navy that the admiral Themistocles had created using the Athenian silver mined at Laurium.

In those days, as in our own, empires had to engage in international trade to buy provisions that made urban life in their capitals possible. In the case of 5th Century Athens, much of the food supply required to feed ever larger numbers of Athenians was grown in the fertile fields of Egypt. This fact presupposed a busy commerce between Athens and the Egyptian ports. By relying the analysis of undersea remains, archeologists have been able to point to an increase in Aegean maritime traffic by a factor of four in the between the 6th and

4th Centuries BCE.[33] By the 5th Century, and probably a bit before, those Athenians playing the role of banker could provide a ship's captain with a note that would guarantee payment in specie (in this case probably the silver coin known called the "Owl") upon delivery of the goods. One such banker was a slave called "Pasion." Pasion created a banking empire for his owner during the 4th Century BCE and died not only rich, but also a free man.[34]

From the days of the Roman Republic through the long rule of the Roman Empire that followed, the Romans controlled the political and commercial affairs of a territory even larger than that of the Hellenic and Persian empires that had gone before. The Roman Empire reached its greatest extent under the Emperor Trajan (98-117 CE) at which time Rome stretched from cold and rainy Britain all the way to the steaming riverside towns and cities of Mesopotamia and covered an area in excess of 2 million square miles. Unlike the Athenians who had briefly enjoyed the rewards of empire a few centuries before, the Romans did not possess a silver mine that they could turn to when the Republican or Imperial Treasury ran out of cash.

---

[33] Strong supportive evidence based on comparing coin hoards has been provided by Roebuck, Carl, "The Grain Trade Between Greece and Egypt", *Classical Philology*, Vol. 45, No. 4 (Oct., 1950), pp. 236-247. Roebuck's evidence shows that, in addition to Athens, Corinth, Aegina, and other Greek city states also fed themselves on Egyptian grain.

[34] Much that is written of Pasion's life and achievements is derived from a single speech by one Apollodorus in an Athenian court case. See: Cohen, E. Edward, "Athenian Economy and Society: A Banking Perspective". Princeton: Princeton University Press, 1992.

Neither did the Italian economy enjoy such agricultural abundance as did the rich fields of Egypt. Finally, the Roman Empire did not produce substantial riches through trade, and manufacture as had some of the Greek city states in the earlier Classical period.

As a consequence of all this, the Senate of Rome and later the twelve Caesars are to be remembered more for their ingenuity in devising taxes than for creating an economy capable of producing wealth. One of the most important ways of filling the state treasury was with the proceeds of conquest, in other words. the spoils of war. The spoils of war included not only gold, silver, and other forms of material wealth, but also ready money derived from the sale of those human beings, usually women and children, who had somehow survived the assault of the Roman legions. In between moments of conquest, however, the most important form of taxation by the Roman state, therefore, was the regular debasement of the Roman *Denarius*. The other form of Roman taxation was taxation itself, namely the collection of taxes from the conquered territories by means of tax farmers, i.e., by those referred to as "publicans" in the Christian *Bible* (New Testament).

Because taxation, rather than trade and manufacture, was the most important form of attaining wealth during most of the late Roman Republic and the early Roman Empire, the administrative dimension of handling money was highly developed during most of the millennium of Roman power.

67

While the activity of loaning metallic currency at interest was carried on by the *argentaari* (i.e., silver dealers) of Rome in much the same way as it had been in the Athenian and Hellenistic empires, the Roman preference for concluding business deals with actual physical money (however debased) inhibited the growth of banking in the full sense.

Bankers, after all, are those who offer the convenience of paper currency in the form of "promises to pay" instead of a metallic coinage that is heavy to carry and easily stolen. Bankers are also, however, those canny businessmen who regularly issue promises to pay amounting to much larger sums than are actually backed up by the gold or silver in their vaults. On this definition, the first "banker" was the man who discovered that no matter how much or how little gold and silver he guarded in his vaults, those to whom it belonged never (or almost never) all came in to claim it on the same day. The Romans, however, were different. In his brief but brilliant *The Ancient Economy*, the noted classical scholar M.I. Finley writes of imperial Rome that:

> This was a world that never created fiduciary money in any form, or negotiable instruments. Money was hard coin, mostly silver, and a fair amount of that was hoarded, in strong-boxes, in the ground, often in banks as non-interest bearing deposits.[35]

---

[35] Finley, M.I., *The Ancient Economy.* Berkeley, California: University of California Press, 1973, p.141.

In his discussion of Roman monetary matters, Finley also points out that physical records (e.g., account books, ceramic tablets, papyrus notes) that might show that there was significant lending of money at interest in Roman times are in very short supply. The whole argument about Roman banking practice, according to Finley, rests on a single tattered papyrus document describing the finance of a maritime voyage from Egypt to Rome.[36] In short, while the Romans may have lent money at interest in the form of actual physical gold and silver coins, they never really developed banking. As long as there were abundant sources of gold and silver available in kingdoms yet to be conquered, the Romans seem to have preferred hard cash to "promises to pay."

Market transactions carried out in the absence of paper money continued when, in 328 CE, the Roman Empire (later to be called "Byzantium") moved east to what had been the small Greek port of Bizantos on the Bosporus, a narrow waterway joining the Aegean to the Black Sea. After that, it was business as usual from the founding of Constantinople by the eponymous Constantine until the arrival of the Turks (and a very large cannon) in 1453 CE. In the feudal era that followed the departure of the capital of the Romans from its original site, most western Europeans had to learn how to do without cash

---

[36] For a more complete discussion of this document from the point of view of an economist, see: Temin, Peter, "A Market Economy in the Early Roman Empire", *The Journal of Roman Studies*, Vol.91 (2001), pp. 169-181.

almost entirely. Banking then became an activity that may have touched the lives of princes and wealthy merchants on the great occasions of war and commerce but almost never the daily life of the common folk.

The Italian Renaissance and the Fortunes of Banking

As we shall see, it was the cruel and avaricious French King known as "good looking Phillip" (*Philipe le Bel*, 1245-1285 CE) who burned a large number of Knights Templar alive to get them to stop functioning as medieval Europe's only bankers. With the destruction of the Templars, the economic space required for the development of something much more like the commercial banking of today was opened up for the ambitious and clever money merchants in the city states of Florence, Genoa, Venice, and many other cities located in the northern regions of the Italian peninsula.

Western Europe as a whole experienced a rapid expansion of economic output in the 12th and 13th Centuries.[37] The rapid growth of output and the consequent growth of European cities, according to economic historian Carlo Cipolla, was due to in part to the maturing and extension technological changes introduced across Europe after the fall of Rome. These

---

[37] *The Cambridge Economic History of Europe.* Vol. III "Economic Organization and Policies in the Middle Ages." Postan, M.M., Rich, E.E, and Miller, Edward, Eds. Cambridge: University Press, 1963, pp. 66-70.

included : water mills; the horse collar; the three field system; and the horse shoe. The sudden increase in economic growth that occurred towards the end of the feudal period enlivened both business and the arts in the Italian city states. The sudden economic growth of Florence, Milan, and Venice, *inter alia*, was also due to that mysterious and inexplicable spirit of creative economic energy which darts around the world and transforms life in a given region only then to leave that region behind and to settle in another.[38]

One way in which the technological changes introduced earlier in Western Europe matured in the late medieval period, Cipolla says, was in the application of wind power. The power of the wind harnessed by the new methods was much greater than the power that had been produced by flowing water that had been primarily used to grind grain. Thus, the windmill (now adapted to turn on an axis so as to catch the prevailing breezes) was then applied to manufacturing processes including: throwing silk; fulling cloth; making gunpowder; dressing leather; extracting oil, and, even grinding mustard.[39]

Both reflecting and driven by such motors of economic change, Northern Italy experienced a rapid expansion of manufacture, banking, and long distance trade in the 14th and

---

[38] Cipolla, Carlo, M., *Before the Industrial Revolution: European Society and Economy, 1000-1700*. New York: Norton, 1976, p.169. Thus, the creative economic energy that transformed the Italian towns in the 14th and 15th Centuries soon departed for England and Holland where it settled in for the following two centuries before departing for the New World.

[39] Ibid., p.164.

15th Centuries. Genoa, Lucca, Siena, Milan, Piacenza, Pisa and Venice all became busy commercial and financial centers in this period. It was, however, the Tuscan city of Florence that seemed to rise above the others; not only in the number of bankers operating there but also in the creation of art, architecture, literature, and learning.[40]

During the late medieval period, the manufactures of the northern Italian cities, especially textiles, began to find enthusiastic buyers not only in the great annual trade fairs of Champagne in France, but also as far away as England and in the Flemish lands of continental Europe where the city of Bruges was the chief commercial and banking center. Wherever such markets required financial expertise and ready capital, there the "Lombards" (who are still remembered by "Lombard Street" in modern London's financial district) could be found.

For reasons that have caused the historians of Europe to write many long and interesting books, many of the cities of "Lombardy", or northern Italy, were not the sleepy autocracies dominated by lubricious dukes celebrated in nostalgic opera such as Verdi's *Rigoletto*, but were, rather, vibrant democratic societies that competed vigorously with each other- not only in the commercial and financial sense but, when necessary, on the

---

[40] Parks, Tim, *Medici Money: Banking, Metaphysics, and Art in Fifteenth Century Florence.* New York: Norton, 2005. See *Cambridge Economic History, Op.Cit.,* pp. 75-76, for a list of ten of the most active north Italian cities and the number of banking companies in each. Florence had no less than thirty-eight banking firms at this time including the Bardi, Perruzi, and Medici families mentioned here.

field of arms. Theirs was the age of the *condotteri*, a professional soldier with an army of mercenaries at his back who chose as his enemies whichever democratic city, ambitious duke, or subtle papal legatee combined the possession of ready cash with the willingness to spend it liberally in the struggle for power. The constant small wars of this period made life hell for the common people, of course, but also provided an attractive, if risky, nursery for the banking profession.

Genoa and Venice were both busy port cities during this time. Ship captains headed for London, Bruges, Barcelona, or Byzantium from the harbors of either of these cities needed financing for their ships and cargoes. As late medieval manufacturing and trade began to grow, those who made their living trading metallic currencies, as had the *argentaari* of ancient Rome before them, then entered the profession of banking by means of perfecting two very important functions. These were: 1) holding the cash collected by the local representatives of the Church of Rome for safekeeping; and, 2) the finance of a new and fast growing international maritime trade. The economic importance of the banking in these cities was attested to by the fact that three of them minted their own gold coinage within years of each other. In the year 1252 Genoa and Florence both struck gold coins called the "*Genovini*" and the "*Fiorini*" respectively. In 1284, Venice issued the gold "ducat" so often mentioned in the plays of Shakespeare. The Florentines, like the Athenians before them, never diminished the precious metal content of their basic currency. The result of this unusually responsible monetary policy was that the florin came to serve as the principal trade coin and unit of account for economic transactions in centers of shipping, trade, and finance all across Western Europe.

There was, however, a major problem that stood in the way of an unlimited expansion of credit and the growth in long distance trade that the efficient banking of the Lombards had made possible. The problem that faced the entire European financial sector at this time was that, according to the Church of Rome, lending money at interest was a sin. This sin was called "usury", and some very complicated foreign exchange maneuvers, generous giving of gifts, and. no doubt, the relatively recent invention of double entry book keeping all helped to keep the holy hounds of the Inquisition off the bankers' backs.

One basic maneuver was to send an order of payment to, for example, London stated in "pennies" (the Florentine *Piccolo*). These *Piccoli* were to be exchanged for Pounds Sterling at a rate that would provide extra coins when the English currency came back home, either physically (not often) or on paper.[41] Not surprisingly for the city which had issued a coin that dominated the commerce of a whole region, Florence was also the city where the art of banking was most highly developed. Although the Medici name resounds most loudly in histories of the period,

---

[41] Cipolla, *Op.Cit.* p.186.

the Medici were still involved in the woolen trade or changing coins on the Rialto when the banking families of the Bardi and the Perruzi dominated Florentine banking in the 13th and 14th Centuries.

Both the Bardi and the Peruzzi grew powerful not only by serving local Florentine business, but also by maintaining banking offices in many other cities around the Mediterranean and in Western Europe. At the same time, both the Bardi and the Perruzi served as the bankers of the Papacy wherever they did business. The largest international organization in Western Europe in those days was, of course, the Church of Rome, and one of its most important activities was collecting the small change of the faithful on Sundays and holy days throughout the year. Clearly, such an institution needed bankers, and both the Bardi and the Peruzzi were only to eager to provide His Holiness the Pope with their services. Apart from piling up credit in heaven by so doing, the Bardi and Perruzzi bankers were able to use the holy funds deposited by the church as their own banking reserves for years at a time. About the only thing that impeded the progress of the Bardi and the Peruzzi to greater and greater wealth was something mentioned earlier we called "the temptation of the Prince."

Earlier governments, for example those of the "Twelve Caesars", had been subject to the "temptation of the prince", which was the urge to recall the coin of the realm for re-minting on regular occasions. Part of the re-minting process, of course, would be the subtraction of a certain portion of the precious metal content of the previous issue of the coinage so that a few ingots of pure gold and pure silver could be put aside for the ruler's use. Scholars believe, indeed, that the various Roman emperors who engaged in this practice regarded the regular debasement of the currency as a legitimate form of taxation.

In late medieval times, however, the "temptation of the prince" had evolved into a new way to exploit the business community. The "prince's temptation" in late Medieval or early Renaissance times, was simply to default on loans taken out from his bankers thus allowing his unfortunate money merchants to fail. For example, both the Bardi and the Peruzzi contributed to the war chest of England's Edward III (1312 - 1377 CE) when he was in need of funds to undertake what ultimately became the Hundred Years War. The Bardi lent King Edward 900,000 gold Florins while the Peruzzi loaned him another 600,000 of the same. It goes without saying that they never got them back. Both old and highly respectable banking houses failed and it was then left to the Medici to take over both the banking and the politics of their native Florence which city they both dominated and beautified for several centuries.

A young man from the Hapsburg dominions in Austria who acquired his business skills as an apprentice to a merchant in Venice learned his profession quickly while, at the same time, carefully observed that city's bustling banking scene. This man, an Austrian, was called "Jacopo" for many years afterwards in recognition of his Venetian sojourn. This intelligent apprentice who was to became one of Europe's most powerful bankers was Jacob Fugger. Another very important thing that the young "Jacopo" learned in Venice concerned the importance of a successful banker's relationship to the Papacy:

> It is shortly after the Medici disappeared from the European arena of financial activity that we first meet the Fuggers in relationships with the Papal See. From the end of the fifteenth century, these relations became much closer, reaching their height under Jacob Fugger in the first decades of the sixteenth century.[42]

During the later 15th Century and throughout the century that followed, the Fuggers of Austria replaced the Medici of Florence as the most powerful bankers in Europe. Like the Medici before them, the Fuggers, who had begun their business life in textiles, amassed great wealth by acting as bankers to the Pope of Rome. The Fuggers also financed powerful princes like the Hapsburgs who dominated central Europe, and who later came to rule the Flemings, the Dutch, and eventually even the

---

[42] The story of the Fuggers and their rise from mining to imperial finance is told by Jacob Streider in his *Jacob Fugger The Rich*. Archon Books, 1966. The book is an interesting and uncritical history, and is dedicated to: "His Highness the Prince Karl Ernst Fugger-Glött."

Spaniards. Thus it was a Hapsburg prince, Charles the First, who came to sit on the Spanish throne lately occupied by Ferdinand and Isabella, a development that turned out to be rather a good thing for the Fuggers.

As noted, the Fuggers had begun their banking interest after their initial successes in the textile business. The textile industry in central Europe had benefited by some of the same technological and economic forces that had spurred an economic an artistic renaissance in the northern Italian cities. Using the wealth that they had amassed in this way, the Fuggers made a loan to a Habsburg archduke in 1487. What then followed was that His Excellency offered the Fuggers a part interest in a mine that he happened to own. This mine, as it happened, produced both silver and copper. This acquisition gave the Fuggers their own supply of two out of the three metals that many Europeans still used as money. They were not slow to take advantage of this opportunity. The year 1519 was a crucial one for the Fuggers, and for their chief client happened to be Maximillian, the Holy Roman Emperor. The news in Europe was that Maximillian wanted to put own his grandson, Charles, on the Holy Roman throne. Perhaps more important for the Hapsburg family fortunes, however, was the fact that 1519 was also the year in which, far away in the New World, a Spanish adventurer named Hernán Cortés transformed a raid for gold and slaves into the conquest of an empire.

The year 1519 was the one in which Cortés, was specifically instructed by the Governor of Cuba, Don Diego de Velasquez de Velar, to trade for (or otherwise acquire) gold, while, at the same time, capturing many slaves possible so as to ease Cuba's troubling labor shortage. Cortés, who had been Governor Velasquez's right hand man during the conquest of Cuba, was also instructed to come straight home as soon as he had a number of human beings for sale and some golden treasure to pile up at the Governor's feet. By then, however, Cortés had decided it was time to conquer some territory for himself. Consequently, by first ignoring and then openly confronting the Governor of Cuba, Cortés led his *conquistadors* to Tenochtitlán, the capital of Montezuma's Mexican empire. There Cortés and his men discovered that the houses were not, in fact, made of gold as they had been told by a wily native chief who had very badly wanted Cortés and his canons out of his territory. Undeterred, by the lack of gold buildings, Cortés and his followers instead discovered the largest and most productive silver mines ever known.

As it happened, therefore, it was to be Maximillian's grandson Charles, known to history as "*Carlos Primero*" of Spain, who then was first to benefit both from the money of the Fuggers which secured him the title of Holy Roman Emperor, and later even more from the adventures of Hernán Cortés. What had happened was that Cortés, despite his original insatiable hunger for gold, eventually conquered a land that,

79

while producing very little in the way of gold, provided a marvelous bounty of silver that flowed in ever increasing quantities into the coffers of the Spanish Hapsburgs to be managed by the Fuggers and other bankers.

The techniques that had made not only the Fuggers but also many other famous banking families incredibly rich during this period included not only the finance of international trade, and making loans to the politically powerful, but also sophisticated ways to get around the church of Rome's prohibition against usury. To do this required extensive international organization and close friendships with the lords of the land. Such relationships suffered when the Prince was too greedy or the bankers were too cautious. However, good banker-client relationships were extremely profitable when both understood each other well, and each hoped to benefit from the other's happy and powerful state. Lending to kings and emperors could be very profitable and rates of interest as high as 45% have been recorded.

The problems presented by the sinful status of the usurer and his anticipated further residence in Hell were, therefore, usually side-stepped in practice. For one thing, the requirement to use different coinage systems in the process of conducting international trade yielded a profit when the rates of exchange were favorable. When the rate of exchange were not favorable, however, the banker simply accepted large and expensive "gifts" from his clients. Such "gifts" could be glossed over conveniently on the opposite side of the ledgers set up using the "double entry book keeping" that had been most conveniently developed in the busy banking and commercial Italian cities of the 13th to the 15th centuries.

Even when protected and profitable, however, the banking companies established on the family model like those of the Medici and the Fuggers eventually either lost creative energy or simply failed economically. For this reason, to protect the manufactures and trade of any particular region from the losses that could be occasioned by the destruction of a family bank, the late medieval state and/or city governments eventually realized that it would be a good idea for the state to step in with its own bank whenever private capital failed.

It was for this reason the *Banco della Piazza di Rialto* was founded by the Venetians at the very end of the 16th Century (1584-1587). This was probably the first bank ever set up by the power of the state. The whole point of its' creation, moreover, was to put the economic resources of the city state to work to protect the manufacture and trade of the community from the bankruptcies in private banking that inevitably occurred.

The Venetian central bank, like any other bank, was set up to provide a secure resting place for the wealth generated by the business people of the city. The basic capital acquired in this way then functioned as a reserve that would make possible the necessary financial transactions (making loans, issuing orders to pay, and financing the maritime trade) that were required to keep the city not only solvent but also prosperous. Because the power of the Doge of Venice stood behind it the, *Banco della Piazza di Rialto*, made it possible for Venetians to engage in their business activities without the inconveniences that came along with a metallic currency. This allowed them to do business more and more exclusively on the basis of transactions almost entirely limited exchanging of pieces of paper.

The founding of the *Banco della Piazza di Rialto*, then, opened up a new chapter in banking history with the creation of what, today, we would call a "central bank." Similar banks were created in other countries in the centuries that followed. However, the whole fascinating story of central banking that began in Venice was soon to be repeated as a tragedy in 18th Century Paris, an not much later to be continued almost as farce in the story of the First and Second Banks of the United States. Finally, after J.P. Morgan had stepped in to rescue the US dollar on no less than two occasions, there occurred the creation of the US Federal Reserve in 1917. All of this, along with a closer look at a phenomenon that we shall call "mass financial hysteria", will be described and analyzed in Chapter 7 that follows. Before doing so, however, lets put the fascinating story of the *Banco della Piazza di Rialto* and its fabulous reserves of gold ducats to one side for the moment so as to take a look at some very substantial reasons for holding gold in our own day.

Chapter 4   When Should I Buy Gold?

As suggested earlier, past history shows that people rush to acquire gold when economic, military, or natural disaster threatens. When all else fails, there is always gold to import food, to go to war, or to respond to hurricane, flood, or earthquake damage. Fortunately, not all of these threats are present at all times, however the possibility of economic breakdown and/or of increasing military tensions are very real. The question "When should I buy gold?" is, therefore, one that may be answered by pointing to the following things:

- the management (or mismanagement) of the domestic economy
- the turmoil in world markets
- possible sovereign defaults
- the threat of war.

We can begin the process with a simple review of the day-to-day function of the gold markets, and then go on to some more unusual factors that have moved the price of gold in the past.

Factors That Influence the Price of Gold

The first part of the answer to question "When should I buy gold?" has to do with the factors that normally influence the movement in gold prices in commodity markets around the world today. These factors are more strictly economic in nature.

They will be examined more closely in the final chapters of this book.

However, they may be briefly stated here as follows:

- the rate of inflation
- the exchange rates of a number of national currencies
- the state of equities and commodities markets
- the possibility of sovereign default

The shortest possible answer to the question "When should I buy gold?" concerns the first element in gold prices given on this list. The **rate of inflation** is the single most important factor influencing the price of gold. The reason, as once stated by economist, John Kenneth Galbraith, is that: "...as a matter of fact, the Treasury cannot print gold." In other words, governments may produce endless quantities of paper money, but the production of gold requires the expenditure of serious amounts of labor and capital. Thus, when the production of paper currencies outstrips the production of goods in any particular country the result is inflation. If you are holding gold, the value of the commodity that you are holding will rise as the value of the paper money (or if you prefer, digital money) that you are holding falls. This is what we call "inflation." The first answer to the question "When should I buy gold?", therefore, is that gold purchases are always a good idea when it appears that the rate of inflation is increasing.

There are two basic measures of the inflation rate that are computed from the Consumer Price Index (CPI) today. One is the so-called "headline rate" of inflation which looks at the whole range of things that we must buy to get through life. There is also the "core rate" of inflation which is computed by leaving food and energy prices out of the calculation. The latter computation is allegedly done to remove the highly variable costs of energy products and food out of the equation to give a more "realistic" figure. Most people, however, will want to know what the general or "headline" rate of inflation is because this tells them is what it is going to cost them to live. It is also the rate that is likely to increase the most quickly and will, therefore, be the more powerful influence on the price of gold. Anyone who is prepared to do the calculation should consider the likelihood of a future inflation that might be produced by any (or all) of the following factors:

- deficit spending,
- increases in the import bill due to a weakening dollar
- sudden and significant changes in foreign exchange rates.

Thus, if and when the exchange rates of national currencies suddenly begin to vary unexpectedly, it would also a good time to think about buying some gold. An example, will make this point a bit more clearly. When, for example, in the late Spring and early Summer of 2010, both the British Pound and the Euro began to lose ground against the dollar, the price of gold registered increases almost immediately. The reason for this was that many people holding those currencies feared serious economic loss and began to move some of their wealth into gold as a "safe haven."

Given this kind of performance of a foreign currency, it is not hard to imagine those holding the currency trying to seek refuge from the economic storms around the Euro by seeking a safe harbor in gold. Finally, there is the troubling question of sovereign default. A sovereign default takes place when countries stricken with failing economies default on their debts to international lenders. When this happens, the gold price can move upwards very quickly. This happens because of fear to the effect that certain countries may be on the point of suspending payment on the debts owed to their creditors.

The following chart shows how much the Euro, for example, lost to the US Dollar in 2010:

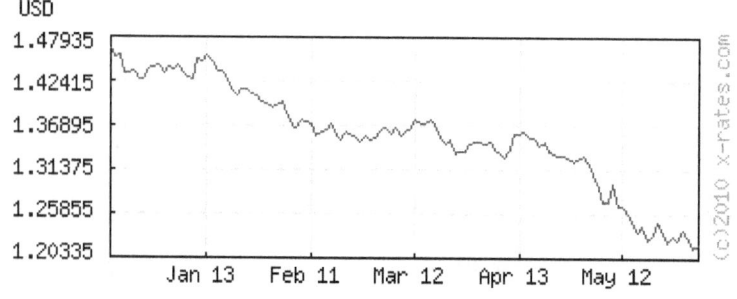

Euro Sinks to $1.21 Against the Dollar[43]

---

[43] Sourced at: http://www.x-rates.com/d/USD/EUR/graph120.html

Finally, there is the troubling question of sovereign default. A sovereign default takes place when countries stricken with failing economies default on their debts to international lenders. When this happens, the gold price can move upwards very quickly. This happens because of fear to the effect that certain Thus, the Greek debt crisis that unfolded in the Spring of 2010 was accompanied by sudden and significant upward movements in the price of gold. What the possibility of sovereign default threatened in this case was nothing less than the collapse of the Euro. This possibility was widely feared as the public debt of economically stricken EU members like Greece, Spain, Portugal, and Ireland was weighed against the economic strength of the more economically resistant countries such as Germany. The "take home lesson" here is that if and when it appears that certain countries are on the point of telling their creditors that debt payments will be suspended it would also be a good time to consider the purchase of gold.

Similar comments may be made about the ups and downs of prices in the equities market, namely the market for stocks and bonds. For many long periods in recent market history equities markets in Europe and North America offered the spectacle of a regular and reliable upward march of the Dow Jones Industrial Average (New York), the FTSE (London), the DAX (Germany) and the CAC (Paris). Under these conditions, nobody was worried about the financial system or the banking sector in these countries. Things have changed. Since the onset of the financial crisis late in 2007 and early in 2008 large scale changes in the above mentioned stock market averages are seen on a daily basis. At the same time there has been a significant decline in bond yields. In the past, investors used to flee an unstable stock market by going into bonds. Not any more. When both the stock markets and the bond markets around the world are looking somewhat anemic, then, it might also be a good time for you to start thinking about protecting some of your savings and/or balancing your portfolio by buying gold in one of the several ways in which this can be done.

Finally, and perhaps most serious of all, is the threat of armed conflict. Not only does war cause the destruction of lives and property around the world, it also interrupts the course of international trade in a serious way. On many occasions in the past, the threat of war caused both individuals and institutions to convert their wealth into gold. When World War I threatened in Great Britain, for example, the amount of gold held in the Bank of England declined from $130 million (July 29, 1914) to less than $50 Million (August 1, 1914) as the British public turned up at the bank to exchange their paper money for coin of the realm.[44] This kind of "run on the bank" is, of course, no longer possible, since we have lived in a regime of "fiat money" for a very long time now. As international tensions rise in the early 21st Century, it is no longer possible to withdraw gold

---

[44] Ahamed, Liaquat, *The Lords of Finance*. London: Penguin, 2009, p.31.

coins from your account at the nation's central bank as early 20th Century Londoners were able to do. At the present time the only way to exchange paper money for gold is to buy physical gold in the form of coins or bars or a reliable proxy (e.g., "paper gold") for gold. Since gold is very expensive, however, and it has become so during the entire first decade of the 21st Century, it would make sense at this point, to wonder just why it is that this shiny and malleable metal costs so much. You may find the answer somewhat surprising and it is to that discussion that we shall turn in the chapter immediately following.

As a final answer to the question "When should I buy gold?", the following information was to be found on the front page of *The Financial Times* as this book was going to press. As *The Financial Times* reporter Javier Blas informed his readers:

> Some of the world's biggest banks and security companies are building vaults to store gold bars and coins worth tens of billions of dollars, cashing in on resurgent demand and record prices. The growing interest in gold among investors worried about the global economy and Europe's sovereign debt crisis has led to a shortage of long-term storage space.
>
> Bankers said that vaulting had become highly profitable. Rising bullion prices translate into higher storage fees, which are usually calculated as a   percentage of the gold price. Gold prices this week rose to a nominal record of

$1,251.20 a troy ounce, up 14.5 per cent since January. Yesterday, bullion [45]traded at $1,226.[46]

The *Financial Times* also reported that some traditional bank vaulting facilities were already full as various banks and storage companies considered building new storage facilities. Whereas the traditional gold bullion storage was a bank vault deep underground, the more modern approach is to create a warehouse like structure surrounded by high security equipment. In a comment that forecasts the discussion to be presented in a Chapter 8 of this book: "Philip Klapwijk of GFMS, the precious metals consultancy, said the move to build more security vaults for gold reflected the "new nature" of the gold market. Investors hoping to benefit from a rising gold price and who are driving demand want long term storage."[47] In the following chapter on how gold is mined and it gold is, therefore, so valuable, we will also learn that there are some investors in gold who make their purchases with precisely the idea of placing it in a vault somewhere.

---

[46] Blas, Javier, "Growing demand for bullion hands banks golden opportunity." The Financial Times, June 12, 2010, p. A1.
[47] *Ibid.*

Chapter 5   The Eternal Search for Gold: And Why Gold Is Still Money

From Scythian Tombs To The Spot Market

Gold as a decorative and symbolic substance has been around for a very long time. Herodotus, who visited the Scythians sometime during the 5th Century BCE, told of the burial customs of these warlike steppe-dwelling nomads. After a long trip through scattered encampments where his survivors lacerated their own bodies in grief, the corpse of the Scythian king would be laid in his tomb:

> Then they strangle and bury in the remaining space of the tomb one of the kings mistresses, his cup-bearer, his cook, his horse-keeper, his attendant, his bearer of messages, and also horses, and a first portion of all things else, and cups of gold; for silver they do not use at all, nor yet bronze in burial.[48]

Much later in recorded history, and after Peter the Great (1672-1725) founded the first museum in Russia in 1714, Russian archeology came into the world with the settled intention to continue the work that their beloved monarch had begun. By the beginning of the century that followed, Russian archeologists had discovered exciting evidence of what Herodotus had reported twenty-four centuries earlier. When a stone burial vault was discovered in southern Russia, the archeologists were both stunned and delighted to discover the

---

[48] Herodotus, Book IV, Chapter 71.

tomb's royal resident was arrayed next to his wife or mistress much as Herodotus had described:

> Around his neck the chieftain wore a magnificent gold torque ending in figures of Scythian horsemen...[and] other precious objects such as an iron sword in a gold sheath...Like her husband, the chieftain's wife had been buried in luxurious clothes decorated with small gold ornaments."[49]

Since discovering this forgotten king (1830), many similar burial sites with gold objects have been discovered in the lands of the Ukraine to the north of the Black Sea on the broad steppes where the Scythians roamed.

In a much more timely use of gold, the Chinese government recently announced that it would be adding more than 400 tones of gold to its monetary reserves. Whereas the ancient Scythians used gold largely to send a beloved ruler and his wife well dressed into the spirit world, the world's fastest growing economy in the early 21st Century is using gold to diversify its financial reserves. As the *Asia Times* reported:

The [China's] 8% growth target has remained the same since 2004 and is also widely seen as politically necessary to create enough jobs to stave off social unrest. While the world's largest economy - the United States - struggles to stem the bleeding of jobs in its ailing economy, its biggest creditor

---

[49] Piotrovsky, Boris, Trans. *Excavations and Discoveries in Scythian Lands.*
The Metropolitan Museum of Art Bulletin, New Series, Vol. 32, No. 5, From the Lands of the Scythians: Ancient Treasures from the Museums of the U.S.S.R. 3000 B.C.-100 B.C. (1973 - 1974), pp. 26-31.

(China) has been quietly increasing its gold reserves in an apparent effort to hedge the weakening value of the US dollar and stabilize the value of its massive foreign exchange (forex) reserves.

One of the key issues that Chinese leaders will have to tackle is whether to let the yuan rise to help restructure the domestic economy and rebalance the global economy. If they decide to allow the yuan to appreciate against the dollar and other currencies, gold may increasingly become an attractive alternative to include within the basket of China's reserves.[50]

What the last sentence cited here implies is that if and when China decides to relax its' "peg" to the dollar and to allow its' currency, the Yuan, to appreciate, then China will have a more powerful currency with which to buy gold, energy reserves, mining facilities, and many other things. The main question that most people not indoctrinated into the mysteries of money markets might ask is this: "Why would China want to pile up gold in a vault somewhere?" This is the question that the present chapter will try to answer. The answer to be offered here is, in part, dependent on a description of how gold is produced, and in, in another sense, dependent on an understanding of the classical theory of economic value. This theory was first clearly stated by one of the best known

---

[50]   Hsiao, Russell, "China assesses its gold strategy", *Asia Times* March 11, 2010.

founders of the American Republic, namely Benjamin Franklin. The short version of the answer to the question concerning China's recent decision to add gold to its monetary reserves may be stated in question and answer form as follows:

Q. Why is China buying gold now?

A. Because it is money.

To understand why this is true it will help to take a look at the processes where by gold has been obtained by gold seekers over the centuries. What Herodotus did not ask himself as he wrote down his report of conversations with the Scythians was why these wandering steppe dwellers used only gold and not silver or bronze in their burial extravaganzas. The most likely answer to this question is also the simplest one. It is that, given the era, and also given the simplicity of Scythian technology at the time, making gold intro jewelry was easier than using the other precious metals.

Gold may be transformed into jewelry and other decorative items when found in almost any of the several versions of its natural state, but is most easily worked into beautiful and/or useful items in the form in which the Scythians were most likely to have found it. This would have been the gold found in the streams and the sand bars that, much later, the California gold rush miners would call "placer gold." Placer gold is relatively easy to separate from the embrace of Mother Earth, and is usually found in a relatively pure state. Such gold may, therefore, be easily transformed into jewelry for the beautification of women, or into the warlike accoutrements beloved of men. Whether we are talking about a gold necklace or golden bosses on a warrior's scabbard, either can be created without requiring the mastery of complicated chemical or metallurgical treatments needed to produce the other two metals mentioned by Herodotus, namely silver and bronze.

The Scythian gold that ended up in royal tombs was, therefore, most likely to have been collected as alluvial or "placer" gold. This the only form in which gold is found not encased in other, more durable, minerals. Placer gold is, therefore, the form that is most easily transformed into useful and beautiful things. This transformation can be effected, moreover, by men using simple tools and even simpler techniques. The other forms in which gold is found, and the techniques by which it is liberated from the metamorphic rock that imprisons it, will occupy our attention in what follows. The descriptions of primary, alluvial, and residual gold will necessitate a brief discussion of the geological principles that are involved both in the location and in the mineralization of gold ore. The whole subject of where gold ore may be found will, in turn, explain why some of the best known "gold rushes" in history (for example the California gold rush of 1849) occurred where they did.[51]

---

[51] Morrell, W.P. in *The Gold Rushes*, London, Adam and Charles Black, 1940, offers general treatment of gold mining beginning in Classical times and

The following brief review of the geology of gold deposits will, in turn, introduce a brief survey of the simpler technologies of gold mining as used in the "gold rush" era, and the more complicated and expensive technologies used by large scale gold mining companies all around the world today. The available techniques for mining gold are utilized both by amateur gold hunters (who still exist in the tens of thousands), or by large and powerful international mining organizations that today can bring both massive machines and powerful chemical methods to the task of finding, mining, and refining gold.

For example, one such organization, the Barrick Gold mining company of Canada, is an international corporation that currently applies many different types of gold mining technology in its 26 mining locations around the world. The amounts of gold currently being produced in the top 50 gold producing countries will also be indicated here together with their contributions to annual world gold production. In the year 2006, for example, total world gold production was 2,310,000 kg. Knowing that a single kilo = 32.1507 troy ounces, some readers may wish to work out for themselves the total value of world gold production in 2006. To complete the calculation, the interested reader may wish to know that the price of each ounce of gold in that year hovered around $600 as can be seen on the chart to be found at the end of this section. The calculation just

---

continuing the 19th Century gold rushes in California, the Yukon, Australia, and South Africa.

suggested, if carried out year on year, would permit a rough estimate of the value of gold brought to market annually.

Gold prices are presently determined five days weekly in gold markets located in financial centers all around the world. Gold market activities start when the sun rises over the sea in Tokyo and Hong Kong, and then continue some hours later with the so-called "London gold fix" before continuing just a few hours later on the NYMEX (commodities market) in New York City. The gold "spot price", as we shall see, is the price of gold for immediate delivery. The spot price is, for this reason, the price that responds (at a moment's notice) to a very wide array of economic forces that will be listed and discussed in Chapter 8 of this book. For the moment, however, the task before us is thesimple and interesting one of learning how (and where) this glittering resident of the Periodic Chart is removed from thefierce embrace of Mother Earth.

Gold Ores and Gold Mining Through the Ages

There are basically three types of gold deposits. They are classified by geologists as "primary", "alluvial", and "residual." Each of these three types of gold deposits are formed by very different geological processes all of which overcome in various ways the rarity of this fascinating basic element. Gold's rarity is estimated at five parts per billion which would amount to about one ounce of gold for each 6,000 tons of rock moved, crushed, baked or leached out of gold ore by the mining company that is in business to find it.[52]

Because of gold's relative rarity in the earth's mantle, special forces of nature are required to concentrate gold in amounts sufficient for human beings to notice it. Several geological processes are required to collect and to concentrate gold in various ways. Gold is brought up from the Earth's mantle by geothermal processes. One example of this would be the powerful up thrust of superheated water that holds the gold in solution at high temperatures and then precipitates the gold out of solution as the water cools. Transported in this way, gold becomes part of metamorphic rocks (e.g., quartz) wherein it collects in veins that can often (but not always) be seen by the naked eye. Closely bound to other minerals, then, gold forms a "primary deposit" this usually being part of a geological intrusion that miners call a "lode" from which the gold must be separated by any number of mechanically vigorous and/or chemically powerful processes.

The easiest type of gold for the more or less amateur participant in a "gold rush" to identify, however, is the type of gold that the "49ers" found (at least for a while) in the mid-19th Century California gold fields. It was alluvial gold that was originally discovered in Mr. Sutter's millrace on a cold January morning in California in the year 1848. Alluvial gold is washed

[52] This figure for gold's rarity is given by geologist Dr. Keith Heyer Meldahl in his historically fascinating and scientifically exact *Hard Road West: History and Geology Along the Gold Rush Trail*. Chicago: University of Chicago Press, 2007, p.xix.

out of the landscape by rushing streams of water along the bottom of which it collects itself into smallish configurations called "nuggets." This occurs when the water in the stream flows in an irregular pattern. Thus, a vortex in the water or the currents created as the stream flows around various rock formations will allow gold particles to sink to the bottom due to their great density (gold is twice as heavy as lead).

What then happens is that the sunken particles of gold compact themselves into relatively small pieces of more or less pure metal by the action of gravity and the pressure of the water flowing over and around them. This was the type of gold that was called "placer gold" by the thousands of mid-19th Century immigrants to California who crossed mountains, deserts, and all the sea lanes of the world in the hope of finding some. Alluvial gold is washed out of its original deposits by the combined actions of erosion and the flow of water towards the sea.

The primary deposits that are the original source of alluvial gold, on the other hand, were created in the first place by the movement of the tectonic plates in a process indicated by the geologist's use of the word "orogenic" meaning "ore creating." The several types of gold that the 49ers found in California had all been created in the first instance by what are called "orogenic" events. Such events included the collisions of tectonic plates leading to the creation of mountains above and strike faults below the surface of the earth. In the case of

California, the orogenic process involved was the "subduction" of the Pacific Plate by the Continental plate with all of the geothermal consequences (earthquakes and volcanoes) that this entailed. The orogenic processes that took place on the western edge of the north American continent included crashes, collisions, and abrasions of the tectonic plates all of which eventually provided the necessary geothermal energy and disruption of the earth's mantle that would result in the creation of various gold ores (e.g., gold bearing quartz, granite and a few others).

The consequences of tectonic collision also included the intrusion of magma or molten rock from below as well as the powerful up thrust of superheated water through the earth's mantle. When these things happened, gold particles in solution were driven into to faults the rock around them or included in the intrusive flows of quartz or granite which shouldered their way in between masses of what the hard rock miner calls "country rock." The orogenic processes just described then collected and concentrated gold particles that would otherwise have been widely distributed through tons and tons of rock. When the gold deposits formed by superheated water and/or magma (along with any deeply buried placer gold created in an earlier geological era and immured in sedimental formations) are exposed by erosion or weathering the gold deposits created in this way are called "residual" deposits. One example of what would be a particularly impressive "residual deposit" would be when there has been a sedimental up thrust of gold bearing sandstone which, when wind erosion has proceeded sufficiently to blow away most of the sand a standing rock or cliff that glitters with tiny grains of gold would be created.

All three types of gold deposits were worked in many of the gold rushes known to history. Perhaps the most dramatic example of a "gold rush" was is provided by the California gold rush of 1848-49. This was an ongoing mining and economic event that put the "Golden State" on the map for the curious, the ambitious, and the unusually optimistic from all over the world. The 19th Century also saw "gold rushes" in Australia and Canada. No sooner were a few nuggets of gold discovered in Mr. Sutter's millrace, however, than ocean going whips were left in San Francisco harbor without crews to sail them as their former crewmen hiked over the land towards Sutter's Mill and the goldfields surrounding it. Chinese workers who had been brought to California (in Chinese the word for California translates as "Gold Mountain") as ordinary laborers also migrated to the gold fields- at first to wash clothing and cook dinner, but then to work the "tailings" (mining waste) on their own account.

At the same time as the clipper ships raced around the tip of South America, brave gold seeking pilgrims were also crossing the mountains and deserts of North America in so as to beat the ocean going gold seekers to California. Both types of gold rush immigrants would soon find all the alluvial gold there was to be found, and within only a few years of their arrival, it would be time to leave again. The process of removing alluvial gold was facilitated by the fact that the techniques for finding placer gold are simple ones that do not require large investments of time or money. Many gold rush participants in California, for example, never got much beyond the acquisition of a shovel and a gold mining pan in these first stages of gold discovery.[53]

Other participants in the California gold rush built sluice boxes. These were slightly inclined open ended troughs in which the waters of a stream washed the heavier gold out of the mud and gravel. Later a larger and more mechanical version of the sluice box was developed and baptized as the "trommel." The trommel was built to include a screen to separate out the larger pieces of rock thus facilitating the collection of gold under the flow of water and, in so doing, accomplished more or less the same thing as the comparatively primitive sluice box but on a larger scale.

In some cases the "tailings", or piles of sand and gravel created in the first stage of gold production, were further worked by late comers using a variety of inventive techniques. Chinese miners in California, for example, are said to have reproduced the technology to retrieve gold from previously worked diggings that had been used originally by Jason and his

---

[53] For a charming photo of one such California gold miner see Meldahl, *Op.Cit.*, p.xx.

Argonauts. The Chinese miners situated blankets in water flowing over the gold mining site in such a way that the fabric of the blanket trapped tiny particles of gold. These were then retrieved by burning the blankets after which the gold thus produced could be taken to the bank. In most 19th Century gold rushes (California, Australia, the Yukon) the production of placer gold would eventually begin to decline. At that point, the more professional hard rock miners would take over the tasks of gold mining while the more amateur mining enthusiasts returned home with (and without) the rewards of mining "placer gold" in their pockets.

Hard rock gold mining involves the discovery of gold bearing rock (often, but not always, quartz) which is then mined as are other minerals. The gold that was found in this way commonly came in veins running through quartz or granite, but could also include placer gold that had been immured in the earth's surface by geological events that had occurred eons before. A late 20th Century California gold prospecting enthusiast explained quite well how it was that the slow but sure processes of geology positioned placer gold not only in the streams or sandbanks, but also much farther up the hillside:

> Eons ago there were many rivers and streams which were concentrating gold before man appeared on the scene. When the Sierra mountain chain was formed by thrusting upward, these rivers were left high and dry. Other streams and rivers formed, cutting directly across the stream beds of the former rivers...It was this gold that the 49ers found. Within a few years

these placers were worked out and the miner who wanted to make a living had to turn elsewhere to find gold. This is when the lodes and tertiary river channels were discovered.[54]

Enthusiastic amateur 21st Century gold seekers still practice both placer mining (largely through gold panning) and the arduous search for hard rock sources in the San Bernardino mountains and in many other California locations. Now, thanks to the magic of video and the convenience of youtube.com, we can visit these hard working amateurs at the click of a mouse. The video recording cited here reveals in its first sequence a thin line of tiny gold nuggets surrounded by a tell tale crescent of "black sand" at the upper rim of a gold pan. In the second sequence, however, the same video shows an even more vigorous form of gold seeking activity. Two strong men struggle with a hillside full of boulders (please note the heavy breathing) in search of gold bearing quartz and other more esoteric gold bearing minerals.[55] In so doing, these amateur gold hunters are recreating the drama of gold hunting in California that first took place about a century before their birth.

---

[54] Black, Jack, *Gold Prospector's Handbook*. Tarzana, CA: Del Oeste Press, 1980. Mr. Black also points out in his handbook that placer gold may be constantly replaced by the action of water. Since his handbook for the amateur prospector was published thirty years ago, it seems to follow that there may be "gold in them thar hill"s once again. Certainly, there are later generations of Californians who think so as will be seen in full color in the youtube.com video mentioned in the next footnote.

[55] The video is provided by an association of amateur gold seekers and is available online at:
http://www.youtube.com/watch?v=4PmWp7Y3buU&feature=related.

Back in those days, the gold panning enthusiasts and/or sluice box operators splashed about in a roaring stream or a burbling brook in the hope of finding all the placer gold there was to be found. Then, after the placer gold began to disappear, the hard rock miner looked for the primary deposits that were the source of the placer gold that ended up in his gold pan. Once these primary deposits were found, the hard rock miner then got busy with his pick and shovel. The strenuous efforts of gold hunting enthusiasts of both types (please think back to the heavy breathing) also offer strong support for the classical theoretical analysis of why it is that gold remains the emperor of the metals. Please welcome the labor theory of value!

Ben Franklin and the Labor Theory of Value

The idea that it is the amount of human labor involved in making things intended for sale (commodities) that gives such things their economic value is a very old one. It was an economist and census taker who served Charles II of England (1630-1685), who was the first English speaking theorist who declared that it is human labor (along with the land that the laborer works on) that causes some commodities brought to market to be worth more than others. This was Sir William Petty (1623-1687) who in a long and varied life served both Puritan and Restoration leaders during one of Great Britain's more exciting centuries.

Sir William did not introduce his labor theory of value as a philosophical or academic exercise. On the contrary, the theory was proposed the potential basis for taxing His Majesty's subjects. Petty credited both land and labor as the source of economic value in his *Treatise of Taxes and Contributions* (1692). In that work the King's foremost economic counselor held that: "...all things ought to be valued by two natural Denominations, which is [which are] Land and Labour." Petty did not spend a lot of time on the labor theory of value in this work, but, rather, left the job of making a complete and rational statement of the theory to a young colonial polymath born in the following century.

Somewhat surprisingly, it was a young North American subject of the British Crown, the Philadelphia printer Benjamin Franklin (1706-1790), who followed up Petty's insight in his "A Modest Enquiry into the Nature and Necessity of a Paper Currency." This was a pamphlet that Ben Franklin published in 1729.[56] In this work, Franklin speaks directly to the problems faced by the North American colonies. The British colonialists of North America, as we learned in an earlier chapter, were condemned to the hopeless task of trying to do business without the benefit of a currency provided by the mother country.

---

[56] A British Marxist who translated Marx's reading notes for *Capital* found a passage in Petty's work which seemed to him to be similar to what Ben Franklin wrote several years later and accused the young Ben Franklin of "plagiarism", but this seems a bit harsh. See Mc Carthy, Terrence, *A History of Economic Theorise: From the Physiocrats to Adam Smith.* New York, Langland Press, 1952. p.XII.

Franklin's concern in one of his earliest works (he was only 23 at the time), was to point out that the mercantilist policies of the British Empire posed monetary barriers to economic development of "the province." Franklin was referring to the province of Pennsylvania which he later represented in London for many years. In his 1729 pamphlet Franklin based his arguments squarely on the assumption that the economic values created by the colonists had been generated by those who labored as husbandmen, craftsmen, apprentices, and ordinary farm hands. Here is what the 23 year old printer and practical economist said about the economic contribution of he and she who labored:

> By Labour may the Value of Silver be measured as well as other Things. As, Suppose one Man employed to raise Corn, while another is digging and refining Silver; at the Year's End, or at any other Period of Time, the compleat Produce of Corn, and that of Silver, are the natural Price of each other; and if one be twenty Bushels, and the other twenty Ounces, then an Ounce of that Silver is worth the Labour of raising a Bushel of that Corn. Now if by the Discovery of some nearer, more easy or plentiful Mines, a Man may get Forty Ounces of Silver as easily as formerly he did Twenty, and the same Labour is still required to raise Twenty Bushels of Corn, then Two Ounces of Silver will be worth no more than the same Labour of raising One Bushel of Corn, and that Bushel of Corn will be as cheap at two Ounces, as it was before at one; *caeteris paribus*.[57]

[57] The young Ben Franklin's pamphlet may be found in the massive collection of his works published by the Yale University Press and available in most university libraries, or conveniently read online with the permission of Yale University who

While the labor theory of value is vigorously condemned in the standard economic textbooks of today, this is probably due to the fact that it was so enthusiastically adopted by the the 19th Century German social revolutionary Karl Marx . rather than for any problem that arises within the theory itself.[58] What Franklin's pamphlet seems to tell us, in fact, is that the labor theory of value is as American as apple pie. By the time that he had reached his 23rd year, Ben Franklin, would have been able to learn of the views of the British economic and philosophical theorist John Locke (1632-1704) who had argued that when men "mixed their labor with the soil", the concept of private property was born.[59]

The man most often credited with being the father of economic theory, however, was the Scottish moral philosopher Adam Smith (1723-1790). What is most interesting for our purposes here is that Smith may have discussed the labor theory of value personally with Ben Franklin with whom he became acquainted when Franklin was representing the interests of the colony of Pennsylvania in London between the years 1757 and

---

have also published Franklin's entire works in digital form. Available at: http://franklinpapers.org/franklin/framedVolumes.jsp

[58] An, unfortunately, very typical argument against the labor theory of value was issued by Joseph Schumpeter in his *History of Economic Analysis*, when, speaking of Marx's version of this theory, simply says that: "Everybody knows that this theory of value is unsatisfactory." Not only does Schumpeter fail to say why what "everybody" knows is true, but, on the very next page, he also says "...it is incorrect to call the labor theory of value 'wrong.'"

[59] Locke, John, *Two Treatises on Government*, 1689.

1775. Introduced by mutual acquaintances, Adam Smith and Ben Franklin became friends in 1759. As a result, Franklin visited the economically minded philosophers David Hume (1711-1776) and Adam Smith in Edinburgh, on two occasions.[60]

Whether or not Ben Franklin discussed the labor theory of value with his two astute philosopher friends in Scotland, we do not really know. A brief look at both Hume's and Smith's pages on economic theory, however, makes this seem very likely. In any case, after Adam Smith took the chair in Moral Philosophy at the University of Edinburgh (1752), he spent most of the rest of his life working on his monumental *Enquiry Into the Nature and Causes of the Wealth of Nations* which was published in 1776. This was the same year in which Smith's friend and mentor, David Hume, died, and in which Britain's north American colonists declared their independence from the mother country. In Smith's, *Wealth of Nations*, the labor theory of value is one of the central themes of Smith's long and fascinating enquiry into the sources of economic growth and the origins of industrial production.

In that massive and still very interesting tome, Smith writes that:

> The value of any commodity, therefore, to the person who possesses it, and who means not to use or consume it himself, but to exchange it for other commodities, is equal to the quantity of labour which it

---

[60] Isaacson, Walter, *Ben Franklin*. New York: Simon and Schuster, 2003, pp.150, 196, 260-261.

enables him to purchase or command. Labour, therefore, is the real measure of the exchangeable value of all commodities.[61]

In his carefully researched biography of Benjamin Franklin, the American historian H.W. Brands points out that Adam Smith was also in full agreement with Ben Franklin concerning the nefarious effects of Great Britain's legislative efforts to keep industry (in this case the iron industry) from developing in the North American colonies. Smith had most certainly been reading Ben Franklin's work, Brands believes, for the author of *Enquiry Into the Nature and Causes of the Wealth of Nations* had not one but two copies of Franklin's 1751 essay criticizing the British government's industrial policy in his library.[62] It is quite likely, therefore, that in presenting his version of the labor theory of value, Adam Smith began with the labor theory of value theme that he had discussed with Ben Franklin either in collegial conversations with Hume and Franklin, or simply by reading Franklin's works. Another great economic theorist of those late 18th and early 19th Century years, ParsonThomas Robert Malthus, also learned from the great American thinker and scientist, in particular from

[61] Smith Adam, *Enquiry Into the Nature and Causes of the Wealth of Nations.* Book I, Ch.V.

[62] Brands, H.W., *The First American: The Life and Times of Ben Franklin.* New York: Doubleday, 2000, p.246. Franklin's 1751 essay was entitled "Observations concerning the Increase of Mankind, Peopling of Countries, & etc." It was also this essay of Franklin's upon which the economist T. R.. Malthus based his famous views on population and poverty.

Franklin's studies of the growth of the North American colonial population, as we will shall presently see.

In his version of the labor theory of value Adam Smith added an interesting paradox both Petty's and Smith's original insights. In his treatment of the "use value" and "exchange value" of commodities, Smith pointed out very astutely that the things that we tend to buy in the marketplace have both a "use value" and an "exchange value." The "use value" of a commodity, Smith said, inheres in what it is that we do with that item. In the case of a shovel, for example, the "use value" of this implement is that it helps us both to dig the earth and to get the snow out of the driveway. The "use value" of water is, of course, that we need it to maintain life. The paradox that Adam Smith pointed out is that, although the "exchange value" of water is very low, its "use value" is critical to our very existence. A strong contrast, Smith said, is presented by diamonds. Diamonds are a commodity that have relatively restricted use value. The diamond may decorate the finger of a married woman, or draw attention to the bosom of a great beauty, but apart from such cases, the usefulness of diamonds is quite limited.

The only thing that resolves the apparent paradox of "use value" v. "exchange value" Smith maintained, is that the diamond requires much larger amounts of human labor for its discovery and transformation into an item for sale, than water requires which very little. In emergencies, indeed, we may just go to a sparkling spring or rustic well and drink some water whereas diamonds are much harder to come by. Adam Smith believed, however, that it was only in the economic life of the more primitive societies that the labor theory of value truly held. Once industrial capitalism had been established, Smith maintained, the owner of what Smith called "stock" (the tools, equipment, and raw material used to produce goods), would add his profit to the price of goods that his factory or workshop had produced. Under these conditions, Smith believed, the labor theory of value would become less useful for explaining the difference in prices between commodity A and commodity B. Well, perhaps, but Dr. Marx, who had already traced the labor theory of value back to Ben Franklin, disagreed. Marx, however, had also carefully read the economic texts of Adam Smith as well as those of the man whom he called his "master." This was the money market genius, Member of Parliament, and retired country gentleman David Ricardo (1772-1823).

Adam Smith had limited his version of the labor theory of value to primitive societies wherein the members that society would have first hand knowledge of how much time it took the farmers, artisans, and artists of their community to produce their goods.[63] As soon as the capitalist employer came along, Smith said, the value equation would have to have a new element to represent, namely profit. When the capitalist added

---

[63] Smith, Adam, *The Wealth of Nations*, 1776, Book I, Chapter 5.

his "profit" to the equation this would render inoperative the calculation of economic value based solely on labor. Ricardo was not, however, willing to adopt Smith's theory in this restricted form. The reason for Ricardo's reluctance in this respect was that he saw quite clearly that the labor theory of value could be very useful to analyze a number of important economic questions of the day not the least of which involved the British landlords who were, just then, making piles of money by charging elevated prices for their grain thanks to the so-called "corn laws" which discriminated against imported grain.[64]

Ricardo, therefore, retrieved and further developed Adam Smith's labor theory of value. He did this by simply pointing out that what Adam Smith had referred to as the employer's "stock" of machines, equipment, and raw materials had also been created by human labor. In addition, Ricardo maintained, Adam Smith had made a crucial error in confusing the economic value that labor creates in the workshop with the wages that labor tends to receive at the end of the day which are, of course, always much less. For both of these reasons, Ricardo argued, Adam Smith's unwillingness to apply his labor theory of value to the world of the industrial revolution represented a major shortcoming in Smith's theory of political economy.

---

[64] The Corn Laws were tariffs designed to protect the income of British landlords from foreign competition between 1815 and 1846. Introduced as an emergency measure they were maintained long afterwards due to the influence of the landlord interest Parliament.

Ricardo then took a note from his friend Thomas Robert Malthus who, as mentioned earlier, had also been inspired by one of Ben Franklin's essays. In his essay entitled "Observations concerning the Increase of Mankind, Peopling of Countries, & etc.", Benjamin Franklin had pointed out that the North American colonial population had doubled every twenty years. Malthus then used Ben Franklin's statistics to create his famous impoverishment theory. The theory developed by Malthus on Franklin's statistics simply predicts that the lower classes in society will always remain poor because, as Malthus put it, population increases "geometrically" where as the food supply grows "arithmetically." This is another way of saying that increases in human populations are exponential in character whereas the increase in food supplies is merely linear in nature. The result of this discontinuity, Malthus believed, would be that there would never be quite enough food to go around, and that, consequently, those lower down on the social pyramid who insisted on large families would always know poverty. Malthus was also an ordained minister of the Church of England, so that it was quite natural of him to blame the poverty of the lower classes on their reproductive habits. Fortunately, however, things never worked out as Parson Malthus foresaw, even though at the time (and on the basis of Franklin's population statistics for North America) Malthus may have made a reasonably good estimate.

In any case, David Ricardo applied his friend Parson Malthus's idea directly to the British industrial working class, and came up with his grimly famous "iron law of wages." Wages for the working class, Ricardo asserted, would always tend to decline to the level of mere subsistence and for exactly the same reason that Malthus had highlighted in his discussion of the matter. Dr. Marx agreed with both Ricardo and Malthus on this point, and generalized Ricardo's position even further. Marx's theorizing in this respect will not concern us in any great detail here, except to say that Marx adopted and expanded the theory originally developed by Ben Franklin with a little encouragement from Sir William Petty. In his version of the theory Marx chose gold to be what he called the "universal commodity." The "universal commodity", Marx said, is the commodity by which all other commodities may be priced. This was, of course, certainly true of gold in his day when world trade was operating on the gold standard, a topic that is treated in greater detail in following chapters. Meanwhile, the labor theory of value that passed through many hands and over a very long period of time may just give us a hint as to why it is that gold has maintained its role as the Emperor of the precious metals for thousands of years.

The Gold / Money Paradox

It was precisely gold's imperial power in this sense that allowed the last of the great barons of American finance, J.P.

Morgan, to provide the gold that would rescue the American economy (and the dollar) from the "panic of 1893." The economic crisis of that year was the last great depression of the 19th Century. What Morgan did to save the day was to arrange for the loan of a significant amount of gold to the US government to prevent a disastrous run on the US dollar which, at that point in time, was still backed by gold. This historic fact leaves us with an interesting problem. It is an observation no less paradoxical than the one that Adam Smith made when he contrasting the use and exchange value of commodities. This one might be called the "gold / money paradox."

The gold/money paradox may be simply stated as follows. Whereas in 19th Century America, gold provided just enough commodity money foundation to anchor the money supply most of the time, there was, however, never enough gold around to prevent currency crises on those occasions when the American economy hit a big bump in the road. This it did, more or less regularly, about every twenty years throughout the 19th Century. In other words, when the American economy was on the upswing gold (and also silver) remained the basis of the currency as laid down in the Constitution of the United States. However, on those occasions when economic disaster struck the American economy (1837, 1857, 1873, 1893), the public's confidence in the American currency was severely shaken. At such times, as we are about to see, only emergency infusions of gold would prevent the dollar from total collapse.

Even though gold was removed as the basis of the American money supply in the early years of the 20th Century (during the "Great Depression" of 1929-1939), gold nevertheless retained its necessary role in international trade. Following the Second World War, therefore, gold returned to its role as the basis of wartime reconstruction and world trade according to the Bretton Woods Agreement of 1944. All of this will help us to understand a number of interesting things that are taking place in international gold markets at the end of the first decade of the 21st Century. It may be possible, for example, to throw some light on why it is that the Chinese government recently bought some 454.1 tons of gold to add to its monetary reserves.

In following chapters we will look into the gold / money paradox a little more closely. What we shall discover is that the last great robber baron of American finance, John Pierpont Morgan, by providing the necessary amounts of gold at the right moment rescued the American dollar on no less than two dramatic occasions. After his successful efforts to save the dollar during both the "panics" of 1893 and 1907, however, Morgan finally told the US government (and the New York City financial community) that the time had come to create a national central bank. Only such bank would be in a position to step in during moments of economic crisis and, thereby, to prevent things from going from bad to worse. In so advising, J.P. Morgan prepared the way for America's third and last national central bank. This was the Federal Reserve Bank, founded in 1913.

Chapter 6 How Should I Buy Gold?

Buying Physicals

There are three basic reasons for investing in gold and there are, therefore, three basic types of gold investor.[65] The difference in each case is easily seen by comparing time horizons. The first type of person who invests in gold is the one who is in for the long haul. The person who buys gold bullion coins such as the Canadian Maple Leaf or the South African Krugerrand is in this first category.

---

[65] Nichols, Jeffrey A., *The Complete Book of Gold Investing*. Homewood, Illinois: Dow Jones, 1987.

A Canadian Maple Leaf

The person who buys gold bullion coins such as the Canadian Maple Leaf or the South African Krugerrand is in this first category. A negative term often applied to this type of gold investment activity is "hoarding." Since the basic proposition of this book is that rational and foresightful individual might, on some occasions, wish to secure some part of their savings with a monetary substance that has fulfilled money's function as a store of value for something like five thousand years, the somewhat pejorative terms "hoarding" and "hoarder" seem inappropriate for use in this context.

Buying Gold Mining Shares

The second type of gold investor is the one who has a portfolio to manage, and who may decide to balance downside risk by making gold related investments such as gold mining stocks or a relatively new type of investment vehicle known as "exchange traded funds" (ETF). ETFs, which some are already calling "paper gold" are described in Chapter 10 that follows. The second type of investor may be described as a "medium term" investor. The medium term investor is one who is more likely to make various types of investment in gold when returns are good, and to make alternate investments at other times. The portfolio manager is, therefore, looking at the medium time period, since, as has been observed many times by skeptics, there are periods in history when returns on gold are flat or negative, depending on the time period in question.

A very eminent skeptic in this vein is Martin Feldstein, a Harvard Professor and former Chair of Ronald Reagan's Council of Economic Advisors. Feldstein has weighed in on the topic of gold as an investment property with a negative statement on gold. In his "Is Gold a Good Hedge?", Professor Feldstein points out that there are periods when gold's price does not rise with the Consumer Price Index (CPI).[66] This is certainly true, but to be frank, nobody ever claimed this particular quality for gold. What Professor Feldstein seems to be saying here is that the price of gold does not rise like other things purchased by consumers as they go about their daily lives. This is quite true, the reason why this is true is also the main point of the present

---

[66] Published online in December (2009). Available online at: http://www.project-syndicate.org/commentary/feldstein18

chapter. In what follows we will attempt to answer questions as to how you should buy gold- given the nature of your investment aims. What we will take a look at here, therefore, is the dynamics of price changes in gold markets. The aim will be to show why price movements in gold are quite different from the price movements of, for example, the Consumer Price Index which is Professor Feldstein's particular measuring stick.

Of course, as no doubt Professor Feldstein is perfectly aware, there are other types of investments (property for example) wherein prices also fail to reflect the staid and sober upward parade of prices as measured by the CPI. Investments in real property, for example, would be an example, since real property represents still another asset class that does not have much of a relationship to price movements registered in the CPI. In the great housing bubble of 2002-2006, for example, prices for housing went stratospheric while the CPI moved modestly upwards. Then, housing prices fell catastrophically as the sub-prime mortgage bubble deflated.[67] If, however, one chooses periods carefully to make a point, as does Professor Feldstein, then the gold price can be seen to remain flat for long periods as compared to the general level of prices. On the other hand, there are also times when the rate of increase in the prices of gold far outpaces the CPI (please see the chart on p. 123 below).

---

[67] There is a very impressive chart derived from official statistics showing the housing bubble online at:
http://mysite.verizon.net/vzeqrguz/housingbubble/. All gold prices and charts are thanks to kitco.com, online at: http://www.kitco.com/charts/livegold.html.

It is precisely when this begins to happen that gold purchases should be considered.

Given the many factors that seem to influence the price of gold, the fact that price movements in gold can be rapid and even unexpected should not come as a surprise. As we shall see, there are a number of major economic forces that can influence gold prices in addition to the rate of inflation. Professor Feldstein points to several moments during the final years of the 20th Century when the gold price failed to rise with the CPI. This is another way of saying that gold prices can remain stable for years at a time which is, of course, quite true. If the American economy could retreat to the peace and comfort of those years when American factories were humming, when the US balance of trade was positive, or when the US Treasury did not owe $2 Trillion US dollars to China and about the same to Japan, then there would be no reason to follow gold prices now. At the end of the first decade of the 21st Century, however, the US economy suffered from massive unemployment, from housing foreclosures in unbelievable numbers, and from a lack of basic services as state, county, and municipal budgets sank to point zero. To respond to the financial crisis the US government spent a large amount of money saving the banking sector (first), and then more money in an economic stimulus package designed to get the US economy going again.

Professor Feldman's statistical technique is known as "cherry picking." Taking the period as a whole, however, the price of gold rose from a low of $280 per ounce in the year 2000 to a high of $1200/oz. in 2009 before falling back somewhat at the beginning of 2010. Only a few months later, however, the gold price pushed through $1200/oz. once again as equities markets trembled and front page photos in the Wall Street Journal showed the iconic agonized stock broker looking up at the ticker.

Gold's long run price increase over the first ten years in the 21st Century was, no doubt, gratifying to both the long term and medium term gold investor. Those who had purchased physical gold had seen their investment increase by a factor of four. Those who had purchased gold mining shares or shares in exchange traded funds (ETFs) had also done well. However there is also a third type of gold investor whose aims and activities will also be considered here. This is the speculative investor who trades contracts to buy and sell gold in the commodity futures market. A detailed description of how speculators operate in this market will be offered a later chapter. A fourth way to invest in gold caught the attention of the financial press in mid-2010. This was to acquire the shares of hedge funds that invest heavily in gold.[68] Some readers will wish to consult the following graph showing the increase spot gold prices for the first ten years of this century before going on.

---

[68] Sam Jones, "Gold denominated share class are worth their weight for Paulson Clients", *The Financial Times*, June 11, 2020, p.13.

According to *The Financial Times*, a hedge fund manager, John Paulson, made some of the shares in his fund available for those clients who wished to profit from recent increases in the price of gold. The Paulson & Company fund manages $34 Billion for its clients. Paulson was the fund manager whose decision to "short" sub-prime" mortgage instruments before the 2007 deflation of the housing bubble resulted in gains of 590% for Paulson's Company Credit Opportunities fund. Paulson's actions in this matter were later investigated by the US government, perhaps because it seemed that making that much money out of everyone else's misfortune must be wrong.

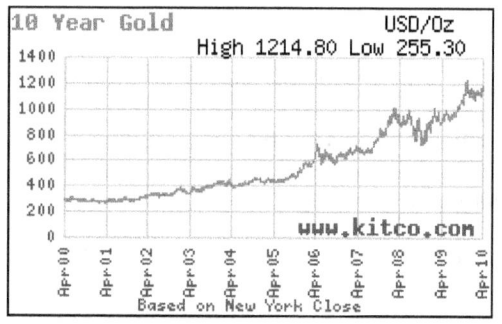

Spot gold prices since 2000.[69]

Be that as it may, Paulson's economic insights more recently led him to create a special part of his fund devoted to gold shares, and he and his investors did very well right through 2010 on the basis of his gold oriented strategy. According to *The*

[69] Image sourced at: http://www.kitco.com/. Kitco sell gold physicals. The Kitco website indicates permission to display Kitco graphs clearly identified as such.

Financial Times, Paulson's fund was up 5.3% overall in 2010. The shares of Paulson's fund denominated in gold, on the other hand, were up 13.5%. It seems that Mr. Paulson has also denominated all of his own shares in the fund in gold. The exact fashion in which Paulson uses his clients money to invest in gold, is by buying shares in exchange traded funds (ETFs) specializing in gold. The ETF is a relatively new type of investment vehicle and will be explained in Chapter 10 that follows. Buying shares in an ETF is a relatively conservative way to invest in gold as is the purchase of bullion coins and gold bars. Both ETF shares and gold bullion coins are investments with a long time horizon. Buying gold mining shares is a medium-term investment and is usually done to balance one's portfolio against downside risk. Finally, speculating in gold futures markets is a very short term type of gold investment that offers the possibility of both profit and loss in your gold investment and is described in detail in Chapter 10 of this book.

Chapter 7   The Rise (and Sometimes   Fall) of Central Banks

The Banco della Piazza di Rialto: Venice 1587

Sources differ on the date of the foundation one of the first central banks in the world. Some report that the Venetian *Banco della Piazza di Rialto* was founded in 1584 while others report the date as 1587. Normally, a difference of three years in such cases can be ignored, but in this case it turns out to be an interesting discrepancy. This is because, upon looking into it, we shall discover that the bank in question was founded twice. We shall also discover that, in between these years, the Senate of Venice argued interminably about banking, much as the Congress of the United States has been doing more than four hundred years later. Why did the Venetians take so long to make up their mind?

The documents detailing the history of the affair seem to show:

> The Bank of Venice not to have been established by gradual development or chance, but by deliberate purpose, in order to take under the guarantee of public authority some of the functions which for two hundred or seventy years or more had been performed by private bankers.[70]

Thus, *The Banco della Piazza di Rialto* was, indeed, founded by an act of the Senate of Venice in 1584. What then followed, however, was a serious battle. On one side stood those who knew that Venice needed a central bank to bail out the private bankers when their speculative fantasies suddenly went from bad to worse. We might remember the Bardi and the Peruzzi of Florence here, but a more timely example might be that of the more recent (2008) Lehman Brothers collapse.

---

[70] Dunbar, Charles F., "The Bank of Venice." *The Quarterly Journal of Economics,* Vol.6, No.3 (April, 1892), p.310.

Be that as it may, the private bankers of Venice managed to keep their own government from founding a central bank for three years. This period ended after, a certain Signori Tomasso Contarino put the case for a state supported central bank so powerfully that the private banking interests had to back down. S. Contarino made his point most forcefully as follows. He simply reminded his audience that there had been more than one hundred banks that existed in Venice: "...of which ninety six have come to a bad end and only seven have succeeded."[71]

Along with the slow and regular growth of banking regulations in Venice, the Venetian bankers had evolved a fairly complete banking system by the time the Venetian Senate took up the question of creating a central bank for the city. The sources show, for example, that the records of the Venetian Senate make it very clear that Venetian banking had evolved to the point that "banking credit" (i.e., written orders to "pay on demand") circulated freely as currency in Venice: "...with such facility as to enable merchants to carry on dealings to an extent otherwise impossible."[72] Thus, by the end of the 16th Century, Venice and the other Northern Italian cities had already achieved what many financial theorists and practical innovators including the Scottish economist and banking entrepreneur John Law (1674-1729) along with first Secretary of the Treasury of

---

[71] Signori Contarino is here quoted by Mr. Dunbar.
[72] Dunbar, p.314.

the United States, Alexander Hamilton (1757-1824), liked to call "the necessity of credit."[73]

Both for Law and for Hamilton, the attempt to manage a growing economy on the basis of a metallic currency alone was reactionary madness. Whereas, John Law was able to make his point forcefully to the French monarchy in 18th Century Paris, however, Alexander Hamilton would have to struggle valiantly, and to make a very interesting compromise concerning the location of the capital of the United States, to establish the "credit" of the youthful republic. At dinner with Jefferson and Madison, then, Hamilton agreed to move the capital of the US from busy New York to sleepy Virginia.

In Great Britain, the Bank of England was founded (1694) on a private basis a little more than a century after the Venetians had established the first central bank in Europe. The Bank of England, however, was purely a non-governmental affair as it was a privately owned joint stock company created with the sole aim of enjoying a monopoly for the purchase of government debt which, following the expensive War of the Spanish Succession (1701-1714) was considerable. Accordingly, the Bank of England opened its doors just after loaning the cash-strapped British government of the day £ 1,200,000.

In the years that followed, the Bank of England, soon to be baptized by the pamphleteers as "the old lady of

---

[73] The adventures of both John Law and Alexander Hamilton will be told in the present and in a following chapter.

Threadneedle Street", struggled to keep her distance from importunate politicians. The idea that the national central bank would function most effectively under the guidance of bankers rather than to submit to the ever changing imperatives of politicians would gain more force as time went on. In his history of central banking between World Wars I and II, author and financial expert Liaquat Ahamed closely chronicles the inter-relationships of the central banks of the United States (the Federal Reserve), Great Britain (the Bank of England), and France (the *Banque Royale*) during the turbulence of the World War I years, and the monetary chaos of Europe in the following decade.[74] According to Ahamed, the challenge for central banking in the interwar period was to manage the national currencies of the European nations most of whom passionately wished to return to the 19th Century gold standard.

This was hardly an easy task given that Germany had been crippled by huge Allied demands for reparations which the Germans were simply unable to pay. These challenges ultimately defeated central bankers in England and France at a time when, following the wartime destruction of the European economies, the United States held most of the world's gold. Finally, all of the efforts of Ahamed's "lords of finance" were completely cancelled during the world wide economic crisis of

---

[74] Ahamed, Liaquat, *The Lords of Finance*. New York: Penguin, 2009.

the 1930s. During the "Great Depression" that unfolded during those years, the central banks of England, France, and the United States largely failed in their efforts to stem economic depression and to get world trade started again.

"Murder! Murder! Rape! Murder! O you villain! What have I kept my Honor untainted so long to have it broke up by you at last?"[75]

 As we shall now discover, however, things were far worse in the early 18th Century when the French first tried to develop a national bank and their British cousins tried something almost as difficult at exactly the same time.

---

[75] Image sourced at:
http://en.wikipedia.org/wiki/File:The_Old_Lady_of_Threadneedle_St.png

The conundrum for central banking in early 18th Century Great Britain was that in times of crisis the Parliament, the Ministries, and even the Monarchy made demands on the Bank of England which would have been disastrous for the nominally independent managers of Bank to heed. Such demands were, however, made in Britain during the period of financial mania known to history as the "South Sea Bubble." The "Great South Sea Bubble" was an exciting and disruptive moment of mass financial hysteria that occurred in Britain during the years 1720-21 despite the moderate monetary policies of the Bank of England. The Bank of England was created in 1694 to enjoy the monopoly of purchasing the government debt. It had, as a consequence, provided its subscribers with a comfortable stream of income since the year of its foundation. The situation in France, however, was very different. The new central bank of France was created by a Scotsman in 1716 and had, therefore, no such staid and sober history.

Two Examples of Mass Financial Hysteria

The first French central bank, originally baptized as the *Banque Royale*, and later called the *Banque de France*, had been imagined for the French Regent, the Duke of Orleans, by a native of Scotland whose name was "John Law." Law was handsome, intelligent, mathematically and financially sophisticated, and also, as it happened, wanted for murder on the island of his birth. Charles Mackay, in his *Extraordinary Popular Delusions*

131

and the Madness of Crowds, begins his account of the events in Paris with fascinating stories about the Scots adventurer and gambler, John Law, and his success in (momentarily) entirely relieving the French government of its disastrous load of debt.[76] This Law did by creating still another company that was intoxicatingly attractive to potential shareholders but a much more risky proposition altogether. Law did this by buying up a defunct state company created to exploit the colonial trade and then turning it into an engine of monetary accumulation.

The original French *Compagnie de l' Occident*, soon to become the Mississippi Company, had been created in 1716. Like the British South Sea Company that had been founded only a few years before (1711), John Law's Mississippi Company combined the fantasy of a monopoly of colonial trade with the sponsorship of the socially prominent and the politically powerful French elite. The excitement surrounding the sale of Mississippi Company shares was generated by the promise of painless acquisition of the riches of the Americas. These were popularly believed to consist largely of gold and silver, precious metals for which the local residents had no use and even less appreciation.

It all began when John Law, a firm believer in the necessity of paper money as a necessary pre-condition for the maintenance of trade, was allowed by the French Regent, to set

---

[76] MacKay, Charles, *Extraordinary popular delusions and the madness of crowds*. New York: Wiley, 1996.

up The Law Company. The Law Company was intended to be a bank in the exclusive service of the French monarchy. No sooner had Law put his bank into operation, however, than he also made available to the French public the shares of the "Mississippi Company." While this company had been originally founded to seek wealth in the French territory at the mouth of the Mississippi, the original company had not made money and had soon languished unto the point of death.[77] When Law bought the company, and when the Regent was known to be backing Law to the hilt, this history was quickly forgotten. As soon as John Law became involved, French investors began to believe that they would now become fabulously rich. By acquiring a company that had been created to enjoy the monopoly of the colonial trade, however, Law was, in fact, copying a similar company that had been created by persons of power and influence in London.

In 1711, the British Lord Treasurer, Robert Harley, had set up a company designed to profit by enjoying a monopoly of a certain part of Britain's the overseas trade. Harley had called his company the "South Sea Company." This company was supposedly established to enjoy a monopoly of the commerce between England and Spain's South American colonies. It was not, however, highly likely that the inventors of the South Sea

---

[77] In one such incident one of the founders of the colony was murdered by his own colonists who were bitterly disappointed when a trip into wilderness in search of gold encountered no gold only hunger, fatigue, and hostile native peoples.

Company actually cared overmuch about trading in foreign parts. Their real purpose in setting up The South Sea Company had been to create a fig leaf for the much more serious business of buying up the British national debt. The monopoly for buying the government debt, however, was a privilege which had already been accorded to The Bank of England only a few years before. Consequently, there was more than just a little bit of fakery involved in setting up a second company to do the same thing.

Then, when diplomatic relations with Spain were severed in 1718, the only thing that was left of the trading concessions that had allegedly been granted to Great Britain was a clause called the "*asiento*" which gave British slavers the privilege of conveying a limited number of African slaves to Spain's American territories each year. In addition to buying up the British national debt, therefore, the mandarins of the South Sea Company profited by trafficking in human lives. Not only was the slaving business quite profitable, the South Sea Company also continued to engage in it- even after the company's shares eventually crashed to the floor.

Nevertheless, for the most exciting and disastrous part of its history, the real business of the South Sea Company was to compete with the Bank of England in the activity of lending large amounts of money to the government in return to a guaranteed stream of payments over the years. The description of just how this concession was granted will show not only how the South

Sea Company eventually finally managed to own 80% of the British Government's debt, but also how, in achieving this privilege, the company sowed the seeds of its own destruction.

As it happened, then, the South Sea Company was a trading company that did not engage in trade overmuch, but rather acted to place the capital of the wealthy landowner and the successful merchant at the government's disposition in exchange for a comfortable return flow of interest payments over time. Since the Bank of England already possessed a supposed monopoly of the same service, the creation of the Lord Treasurer's South Sea Company eventually resulted in a serious Parliamentary battle between two opposed factions within the noble élites of the era.

At first, the subtle and powerful Prime Minister of the day, Robert Walpole, defended the monopoly position of the Bank of England in Parliament. To do so, however, Walpole was required to confront his many wealthy and illustrious opponents who had already invested heavily in the South Sea Company. These notables responded vigorously both in passionate polemic and by quietly applying some of their money where they thought it would do the most good. Some accounts of the affair put the size of the bribery package conveyed to certain members of Parliament by South Sea Company promoters at tens of thousands of Pounds Sterling.[78]

---

[78] Hoppit, Julian, "The Myths of the South Sea Bubble", *Transactions of the Royal Historical Society*,

According to the Scottish journalist Charles MacKay's version of the events , the South Sea Company simply made the British Parliament a more attractive offer than the Bank of England had done. The promoters of the South Sea Company asked Parliament to allow them to increase their capital from £10 Million to £12 Million. This they would raise by subscription forthwith. At the same time the South Sea Company promoters offered to accept government interest payments of five rather than six percent.[79] Then, the wealthy men who were the backers of the South Sea Company used a number of clever tricks to make the shares of the company attractive to the public. In this ploy the promoters of the South Sea company succeeded beyond their wildest dreams.

Important Parliamentarians (and their mistresses), along with a chosen few investors of high status and generally recognized financial acumen, were allotted shares of the company without actually having to pay for them. Then, in a maneuver strikingly similar to the "write to market" moves that made certain corporate executives in the United States fabulously wealthy by means of undated "stock options" during the dot.com boom of the 1990s, those highly born, excessively wealthy, or politically prominent individuals (along with a popular actress or two) had only had to wait until the price of South Sea Company shares rose sufficiently high, to sell the

Sixth Series, Vol. 12, (2002), pp. 141-165.
[79] MacKay pp.70-71.

shares that they had been given by the scheme's promoters and then to quit the game while they were ahead. Whether or not, as Charles Mackay believed, there was some enthusiasm for Britain's South Sea Company that leapt from the excited streets of Paris to the equally clamorous streets of London,

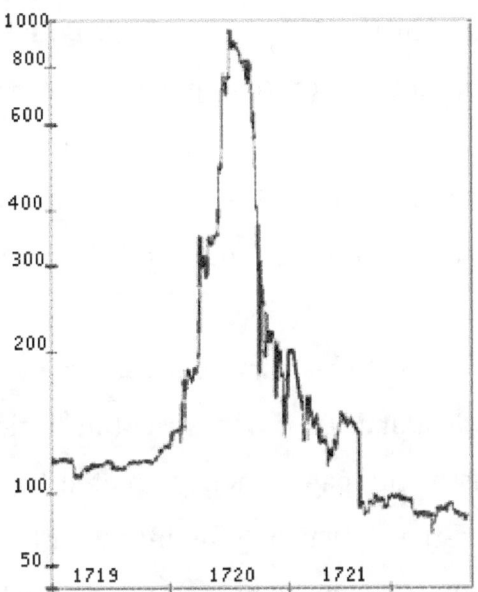

Price of South Sea Company Shares (in Pounds Sterling)[80]

the rise and fall of South Sea Company shares in London during the 1720-21 period show that there were some very powerful influences at play.

Mass Financial Hysteria in Paris

A similar pattern in the breathtaking rise and sudden fall of share prices was also seen in the shares of Law's Mississippi

---

[80] Image sourced at: http://commons.wikimedia.org/wiki/File:South-sea-bubble-chart.png

Company in Paris. John Law was the scion of a successful Scottish goldsmithing and banking family who, as a young man, worked in the family firm and thereby gained first hand experience of banking. Law was also gifted in the art of mathematical calculation and turned his god given talent in this area to his natural inclination as a gambler. Both Law's ability to calculate and his inclination to gamble may be borne in mind while considering the financial miracle that he achieved for his friend and benefactor Philippe the *Duc D' Orleans* (1674-1723) who acted as the French Regent during the minority of Louis XV (1715-1723).[81]

Due, no doubt, to his experience as a youthful apprentice banker in the Scotland, Law was an enthusiastic promoter of "credit" (that is of the paper money created by bankers) and, indeed, believed that it was only by means of the expansion of paper money that the growing commercial activities of the Western European countries could be supported. This seemed obvious to Law, since, thanks to constant war and the extravagance of the French and English ruling classes, "specie", or gold and silver coinage, had a habit of disappearing for foreign parts when it was most needed. After an early attempt to impress Louis XIV 's chief financial minister with his

---

[81] Law's reputation has improved in recent times with more attention paid to his mathematical and financial genius than to his one duel that produced a fatality and his ability to make a living as a gambler. Please see: Kaiser, Thomas E., "Money, Despotism, and Opinion in Early Eighteenth Century France",
The Journal of Modern History, Vol. 63, No. 1 (Mar., 1991), pp. 1-28.

proposals for "expanding credit" and reviving commerce and trade in France, it was the aging "Sun King" himself who said "*Non!*" to Monsieur Law's enthusiastic paper money ideas.[82] The Fourteenth Louis undoubtedly knew that, after his interminable series of wars, there was simply not enough metallic coinage in his realm to support the daily needs of business in any useful way. If the "Sun King" was aware of this, however, it did not lead to any efforts on his part to deal with the problem. Perhaps, by then, the aging monarch simply decided that, since he was the "Sun King" that, after him, "the rain must fall", as indeed it did.

After the *Roi de Soleil* died, however, his nephew, the *Duc D'Orleans*, was only too eager to engage the clever Mr. Law to solve France's monetary problems. For starters, this would mean doing something about the massive government debt that existed after nearly a century of war. Law handled the problem brilliantly and he began by introducing decent banking procedures into French life According to Charles MacKay's account, the Law Company would honor the notes (i.e., promises to pay) that Law issued by handing over coins containing the exact amount of precious metal that had been current at the time that the note was written. This actually made the notes of

---

[82] Some years before John Law had written his *Money and Trade Consider'd with a Proposal for Supplying the Nation with Money* (1705) to support his ideas to the effect that only the widespread adoption of paper money could solve Europe's economic problems. Law had this translated into French when he began to promote his banking ideas in France.

the Law company better than most of the coinage in circulation, since much of the coinage had previously been debased by the Royal government by removing as much of the original content of precious metal as possible. The result of Law's action to honor the notes of his bank in valid coins created a sudden popular regard for John Law along with many popular testimonies to his high intelligence and undoubted financial probity.

Then, no sooner had the Law Company become the *Banque Générale Privée*, and France's first central bank, than Law also purchased the defunct Mississippi Company (1717). After changing the company's name to the *Compagnie D' Occident* ("Company of the West"), Law began to promote its money making potential among his loyal and enthusiastic public. He made his appeal to aristocrats, to wealthy merchants, to ordinary tradesmen as well as to anyone else with ready cash. "Ready cash" in this case included the (by then) nearly useless *Billets d' Etat* (or, "State Notes") which constituted the entire debt of the Royal French government.

The *Compagnie D' Occident* story that was told in aristocratic French drawing rooms, bedrooms, and almost everywhere else, was that the company, soon to be called the "Mississippi Company" would be the vehicle that would, almost instantaneously, transport the incredible riches of the New World back to France. Public interest in the "Mississippi Company" ranged from the lords of the land down to the lowest commoner in France. It was sparked by the dream of sudden wealth beyond the dreams of avarice, and bone aloft like a balloon on hot winds of Parisian gossip. This spark soon ignited an inferno of speculation that strangely resembled the one that was, at the same time, making things hot for the supposedly much more sober British cousins just across the Channel.

The end of the story is much easier to tell than the beginning. In France, a disgruntled aristocrat called the "Prince de Conti" who had been refused the opportunity to acquire additional stock in the Mississippi company, suddenly appeared at the doors of John Law's *Banque de France* with large three wagons. The angry nobleman's purpose was to demand the return of his money in hard cash. The Prince de Conti was quickly and firmly talked out of this spiteful act by a furious Regent. At the same time, however, the more skeptical stockholders began to think about locking in their profits by selling some or all of their shares. In one case, a successful stock jobber who had made a fortune providing Mississippi Company shares to the public, transformed his own shares into gold and silver coin, placed them in a wagon under a large pile of manure, and then, after putting on the smock of an impoverished peasant, drove his treasure across the border into Belgium.[83]

Meanwhile, in Great Britain, a number of aristocratic courtiers who were preparing to accompany the King, George I, on a European tour all showed up at the same time to exchange

---

[83] MacKay, p. 50.

their South Sea shares for coin of the realm. This started a panic among the still hopeful holders of South Sea paper similar to the same emotion that was just then infecting the holders of Mississippi Company stock in Paris. In London whispered stories about the King's courtiers all demanding to convert their South Sea company shares at the same time led to the immediate and disastrous fall in South Sea shares mentioned earlier.

Once the optimism of the bubble had succumbed to the mass fear of the panic, both the French and British investors in the two overseas companies saw a catastrophic collapse in the value of their shares. Some lost substantial amounts of their family fortunes while others were destroyed entirely. Recent scholarly opinion holds that the real meaning of the French bubble was to prepare the common people of France for their tasks in a French revolution that was already in sight along the road ahead. In the process of trying to keep the *Banque de France* from collapsing, for example, the Regent became involved in several standoffs with the French Parliament. This scene provided a dramatic preview of revolutionary scenes like the famous Oath of the Tennis Court that would help to kick off the popular rebellion that would one day cause a later French monarch to lose his head. Meanwhile, the sudden failure of all of John Law's schemes led to violent scenes as French soldiers with fixed bayonets confronted a stone throwing Parisian mob that had gathered outside the gates of John Law's elegant gardens in Rue Quecampoix where, not long before, stock brokers had set up tents to buy and sell Mississippi Company shares.[84]   Dramas of this nature were to be repeated in Paris with far more definite political consequences as the French Revolution arrived to close the 18th Century in a violent explosion of social rage.[85] Meanwhile, just across the Channel, while the South Sea Bubble affair had destroyed the savings of some of the London well-to-do lords and ladies, it had done very little to hurt the basic commerce of the country.[86]

In the end it seems fair to say that John Law's potentially very useful plan for introducing central banking to France had failed in its original purpose.   On the other hand, after the collapse of the South Sea Bubble economic life returned to normal in Britain. In retrospect it seems quite clear that the more sober practice of central banking as carried on by the Bank of England, in fact, provided a far more reliable system for funding the government debt than the schemes put forward by South Sea Company promoters. Unlike Law's bank in France, which had been required to issue additional currency whenever the Regent thought that this might be a good idea, the Bank of England survived the South Sea Bubble madness quite handily. This happy development then left the productive forces of the British economy relatively free to   continue a profitable and

---

[84] *Ibid.*, pp. 57, 67.
[85] Kaiser, *Op Cit.*
[86] Hoppit, *Op.Cit.*

expansive mercantile revolution that would soon transform itself into world empire.

As the histories of two moments of mass financial hysteria in London and Paris seem to show, there are times when it makes sense to ignore the latest financial miracle and to invest something that will hold its value even as major economic problems arise. What we need to do to accomplish this is to identify the problems that might affect financial markets (and hence the price of gold) before such problems actually arrive. What this means is becoming aware of economic danger signals. A list of these will be offered in the following chapter along with a detailed analysis of the dynamics of the gold market.

Chapter 8 How Gold Markets Work Today

Factors of Demand in Gold Markets Today

Because of gold's very long history of being used, first as a commodity money, then as the basic material of coinage systems and finally, as the bank reserves, it is bought and sold in gold markets according to a very wide range of influences. Gold is, therefore, a commodity that has developed a much more complicated structure of demand than more ordinary commodities like coffee, frozen concentrated orange juice, or feeder cattle. The four major types of demand for gold may be listed as follows:

- bankers' demand (monetary reserves).
- fabrication demand (watches and jewelry)

144

- savings demand (bullion coins, gold bars)
- speculative demand (in futures markets).

Since 1987, and the founding of the World Gold Council (WGC), it has been possible to access up-to-date statistics on the demand and supply of gold. The available statistics include the following: 1) country-by-country totals of gold being produced around the world; 2) the amounts of physical gold held by national banks; 3) The amounts of gold being held by commodities exchanges and exchange traded funds; and finally, 4) the amounts of gold used each year in the creation of watches, jewelry and accessories as well as small amounts for more specialized items such as the internal contacts of cell phones, corrosion free surgical implants, and the visor of the astronaut's helmet that reflects the harsh force of the sun back into space.

The World Gold Council is a private association of gold producers which is dedicated to stimulating the demand for gold. The statistics it produces are widely used, and are generally considered to be reliable. The data on monetary reserves presented here come from statistics gathered by the International Monetary Fund and have been presented by the WGC. We can begin with the first of the elements of demand mentioned above, namely bankers' demand. The amounts of physical gold held by the central banks of various countries vary widely as do the circumstances under which this gold might be transferred to other owners.[87]   The United States holds the largest amount of gold in its vaults (8,133.5 metric tonnes) at the highly defended gold depository at Fort Knox in the state of Kentucky.[88]   Given that both Germany and the International Monetary Fund are listed right after the United States in terms of the amounts of physical gold that they hold in reserve, and given that these entities each hold only a little over 3000 metric tonnes each, it seems safe to say that no other nation or international institution comes close to the amount of physical gold held by the United States.   At the other end of the scale, in terms of gold reserves, is Canada.

Canada is a gold producing nation and holds only 3.4 metric tonnes of gold in their foreign exchange reserves. This is a much smaller amount than the amount held by Canada's large and powerful southern neighbor, and smaller even that the amount that wealthy Germany holds in reserve. Even though it is not entirely clear just how it is that the gold in Fort Knox backs the US currency, it might be interesting to note that percentage of US dollars outstanding that would (theoretically) be covered by the Fort Knox reserves of physical gold was

---

[87] A convenient list of the amounts of gold held in reserve by national banks and international bodies like the IMF can be found online at: http://en.wikipedia.org/wiki/Gold_reserve.

[88] "Gold Reserve", Wikipedia. Online at: http://en.wikipedia.org/wiki/Gold_reserve#cite_note-12. A metric ton or 1000 kilograms equals 1.10 US tons.

68.7% in 2009.[89] Although the amount of, say, German foreign exchange reserves held in gold (3,407.6 metric tonnes) may seem large, it is, somewhat surprisingly, about the same quantity of the precious yellow metal demanded for the fabrication of watches, jewelry, and gold accessories in a typical year.

This somewhat surprising fact, then , brings us to the next major source of gold demand. This is the gold demanded for the production of jewelry, watches, and accessories in a single year. According to the World Gold Council, the amount of gold needed for fabrication in 2008 was 2,186.7 metric tonnes. This included the gold needed for watches and jewelry as well as for other items requiring gold such as electronic devices, special industrial applications, and the gold used by dentists to repair teeth. The amount required for fabrication, when added to the amount required to make bullion coins and bars, was 3,805.7 metric tonnes.[90] Thus, the fabrication demand for gold jewelry, gold teeth, and bullion coins and bars for private saving in 2008

---

[89] This proportion is reflected in one of the few jokes that has ever been circulated about a topic as difficult to explain as the role of monetary gold reserves. A native of Kentucky, where Fort Knox is located, grows tired of listening to a Texan brag about how everything is bigger and better in Texas. Kentucky native- "OK, Texas is big. But we got enough gold in Fort Knox to build a gold fence all the way around the state of Texas!" Texan- "You do that boy! And if I like it, I'll buy it!"

[90] "Gold Research and Statistics", The World Gold Council. Online at: http://www.research.gold.org/supply_demand/

was just as large (or a bit larger) than the amount required to back Germany's *Deutchmark*.

The WGC indicates, however, that in the following year (2009), gold fabrication demand was down 11%. This should not surprise us overmuch since, in that year, the world economy slipped into a widespread and profound economic slump. One immediate result of that slump was that both the gold demanded for jewelry and the gold demanded to create bullion coins and gold bars experienced a decline in demand of 20% and 57% respectively. Despite the slump in fabrication demand, however, the price of gold in world markets continued its steady rise as seen in the chart of spot gold prices reproduced earlier (please see p. 125 above).

What the slow and steady rise of the gold price between 2000 and 2010 seems to mean is that the increase of demand for gold during this period emphasized gold's store of value function to a significant degree. In other words, a noticeable number of individuals and institutions had decided that, in case of economic problems yet to come, they wanted to acquire some gold...just in case. Under the circumstances, it may some cause for concern to learn that the output of gold mines all around the world has been declining since the beginning of the 21st Century. In other words, despite the continual rise in the price of gold, the mining companies have actually brought less, not more, gold to the international market place. Why is this?

Factors of Supply in Gold Markets Today: Gold Mining

Many experts have been trying to answer this question. This includes both Dr. Thomas Chaize in his *Energy and Mining Newsletter*, as well as spokesmen for the World Gold Council, and for Barrick, Incorporated, the Canadian gold mining company. Many writers who both follow and comment on the gold market have also noted the surprising fact that the decline in world gold production began at just about the same time that gold prices had begun to rise in world markets. Many commentators still explain the recent declines in gold production in terms of the long lead time required for creating the necessary physical infrastructure to operate a gold mine. This includes the construction of open pit structures, the creation of, roads, towns, and the building of processing and refining facilities all of which are required to mine, to process, and to refine gold. All of this is true and very important given the large expense involved, and yet there is a potentially more troubling reality underlying the general picture of sustained decline in gold production. There are two major problems here. The first is that the costs of mining an ounce of gold are going up. The ores being found are not as rich as in earlier times, and the expenses of preparing a gold producing area for mining are high.

The first problem is already troubling large international mining companies such as Barrick Gold of Canada. Barrick Gold operates twenty-six gold mines in nine countries all around the world.[91]   The underlying problem may, however, may an even more troubling than the increasingly high cost of mining gold. This is that the world may have reached "peak gold" production in the same way that it already seems to have reached "peak oil" production.

The "peak oil" moment was predicted by the petroleum geologist, M. King Hubbert.   Hubbert worked first for the oil companies and later for the US Geological Survey. Using a very simple formula (and the extensive resources of his employers to to get the necessary statistics)   Hubbert   predicted that the United States would reach peak production of oil between 1965 and 1970.[92]

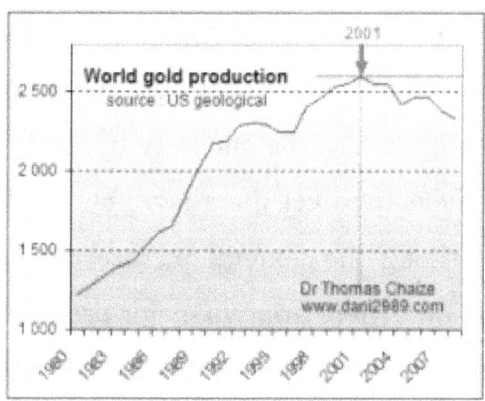

---

[92] The relationship that Hubbert worked with is $T(max) = (1/b) \times Ln (a)$ where b and a are constants representing the amount of estimated reserves and the rate of extraction respectively.

World Gold Production Began to Decline in 2001[93]

In this formula T max stands for the moment when oil production begins to decline. The constant **b** stands for the estimated reserves still left in the Earth. The constant **a** stands for the rate at which petroleum is removed from Mother Earth's ever tighter embrace.

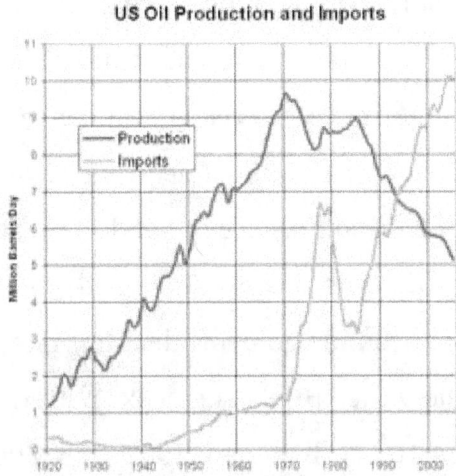

US Oil Production and Imports

M. K. Hubbert's Peak Oil Prediction Right on Target[94]

Hubbert made a "minimalist" and a "maximalist" prediction. Hubbert was right on target for the second of these as oil production in the United States began to decline in the

---

[93] "Gold Production in the World 2009", *Dr.Thomas Chaize Energy and Mining Newsletter.* Available online at:
http://www.dani2989.com/gold/goldprod0509gb.htm.

[94] Image sourced at: http://en.wikipedia.org/wiki/Peak_oil.

year 1970.[95] If the Hubbert peak phenomenon turns out to be as true for gold as it was for petroleum, then the larger international gold producers will also be spending more time and more money to mine gold with every year that passes. At the same time, they will be producing less and less gold. Late in 2009, Barrick Gold's President, Aaron Regent, gave his opinion on this matter to a reporter in London during an important international conference on the future of gold: "There is a strong case to be made that we are already at 'peak gold'," Mr. Regent told a reporter from *The Daily Telegraph* at the Royal Bank of Canada's annual gold conference in London.[96] Statistics presented by the World Gold Federation tend to support Barrick's view to the effect that gold production, like that of petroleum, may also follow the "Hubbert's peak" pattern. Thus, a gold price decline of 10.1% between 2001 and 2009 was followed an increase of the dollar price of gold of no less than

---

[95] An extensive write up on the peak oil view is available online at: http://en.wikipedia.org/wiki/Peak_oil.
According to most sources, peak oil production was reached in the US (1970) within the time frame predicted by Hubbert.

[96] Evans-Pritchard, Ambrose, "Barrick shuts hedge book as world gold supply runs out", *The Daily Telegraph*, November 11, 2009. When gold mining companies report their "hedge" they refer to the amounts of gold they sold at prices agreed upon earlier by means of futures contracts in the way explained on pp.183-4 above. Barrick's sales of gold at prices then far below the prices given in a rising market made enemies among "the gold bugs" according to the author of this article who also reports that Barrick had ceased to hedge gold since the policy had cost them no less than $5.7 Billion in a rising market. Since 2001 Barrick had "hedged" no less than 20 million ounces of gold. The article is available online at: http://www.telegraph.co.uk/finance/newsbysector/industry/mining/6546579/Barrick-shuts-hedge-book-as-world-gold-supply-runs-out.html

221%![97]   World wide gold mine production was 2,476/mt in 2007, 2,409/mt in 2008, and 2,554/mt in 2009.[98]   221%![99] World wide gold mine production was 2,476/mt in 2007, 2,409/mt in 2008, and 2,554/mt in 2009.[100]

Meanwhile, the list of the leading gold producing countries has undergone an important change. China, which has been investing heavily in gold production in recent years, is now the world's largest producer of gold. In 2007 China displaced South Africa from the top spot in gold production which it had occupied throughout the 20th Century. As noted earlier, the Chinese government has been buying large amounts of gold to back its currency, the Renminbi (RMB). Somewhat unusually however, most of the gold produced in China is consumed within the country for the fabrication of watches and jewelry. In 2007,

---

[97] Chaize, Dr. Thomas, "Gold Production in the World (2009)", *Energy and Mining Newsletter.* Available online at:
http://www.dani2989.com/gold/goldprod0509gb.htm

[98] These figures are provided online by the World Gold Council and GFSM, Ltd. and may be viewed after registering on the WGC website. The chart from which these figures were taken is online at:
http://www.gold.org/assets/file/value/stats/statistics/pdf/Supply_Demand.pdf.
"mt" means "metric tons" which is also rendered as "tonnes."

[99] Chaize, Dr. Thomas, "Gold Production in the World (2009)", *Energy and Mining Newsletter.* Available online at:
http://www.dani2989.com/gold/goldprod0509gb.htm

[100] These figures are provided online by the World Gold Council and GFSM, Ltd. and may be viewed after registering on the WGC website. The chart from which these figures were taken is online at:
http://www.gold.org/assets/file/value/stats/statistics/pdf/Supply_Demand.pdf.
"mt" means "metric tons" which is also rendered as "tonnes."

gold output in China increased by 12% over the previous year at which time China produced 276 metric tonnes, of gold. South Africa, which lost its position as number one producer in that year, produced 272 tonnes of gold.[101]   When South Africa moved into the number two spot for annual gold production, many experts who follow gold production and gold prices felt a sudden concern, since this development seemed to confirm the idea held by some to the effect that there is a "Hubbert peak" in gold production as well. The overall picture of gold supply year-on-year has been one in which the quantity of gold sent to world markets by the mining industry, continues to decline.

Gold From "Scrap"

Industry sources tend to refer to the gold that is produced by melting down jewelry, watches, and/or gold retrieved from old computers and other sources as "scrap." There are two interesting things to notice about the production of gold from scrap.   The first is that the amounts of gold produced every year by melting down items made of gold are surprisingly large. The second point of interest is not so surprising.   This is that the annual amounts of gold produced from scrap are highly determined by the market price of gold in the immediately preceding period. Gold production from scrap

[101] "Gold Mining in China", *Wikipedia.* Available online at: http://en.wikipedia.org/wiki/Gold_mining_in_China

in 2007 was 956 metric tonnes which was equal to more than three times the amount of gold mined in China (276 tonnes), the top national gold producer in that year.[102] This amount of gold was produced from "scrap" during a year when the gold price reached $695.39/oz. When the gold price moved up to $871.96 in the following year (about a 25% increase) the amount of gold produced from scrap also increased to 1,217 tonnes (about a 27% increase).

Finally, a certain amount of gold is made available on world gold markets when central banks sell some proportion of their reserves. This happens in most years. In the past central bankers have felt, on occasion, that the amount of gold held in reserve to back the national currency was excessive. At such times, certain central bankers decided to place some part of their gold reserves on the market so as to generate credits in dollars or some other currency. As might be expected, gold supplies from this source seem to be directly influenced by the state of the world economy. In times when national economies come under strain, central bankers in the countries involved are prepared to sell less and less of their gold reserves and at some point central bank sales will cease entirely.

---

[102] World Gold Council. Available online at:
http://www.gold.org/assets/file/value/stats/statistics/pdf/Supply_Demand.pdf, and for Chinese production in 2007, *Gold News*. Available online at:
http://goldnews.bullionvault.com/gold_mining_output_2008_china_south_africa_020620082.

Accordingly, the figures for amounts of gold sold by central bankers for 2007, 2008, and 2009 were 484 metric tonnes, 236 metric tonnes, and 44 metric tonnes, respectively.[103] In other words, as economic and international tensions increase so does the price of gold. This happened recently when:

- the housing bubble deflated in the United States
- unemployment increased in the traditional industrial countries
- tensions in the Middle East and South Central Asia increased
- fears of sovereign default of economically weak EU countries spread.

In such cases, the central bankers of the affected countries were less and less willing to sell any part of their reserves held in gold. What all of this seems to suggest is that there is more than simply supply and demand forces that influence the price of gold. What the economists like to call "externalities" also play a major part. We can take a look at some of these forces now.

War, International Tensions, and the Price of Gold

War and the threat of war has always caused the prudent to place some of their wealth in gold. War means the breakdown of international relations in general and the potential breakdown of monetary systems in particular. War

---

[103] World Gold Council, *Op.cit.*

also exhausts the national treasuries of the countries involved. After the massive destruction of the Second World War (1939-1945), most European nations as well as China and the Soviet Union were present among the 44 US allied nations present at the Bretton Woods conference which will presently be described in greater detail. Following the massive destruction of World War II, most of America's allies were economically bankrupt and were, therefore, only too happy to sign up for membership in the (gold based) Bretton Woods system.

As we shall see, the massive debts incurred by the United States during the Vietnam War (1963-75) were to be a major factor in the breakdown of the Bretton Woods system following upon a massive gold outflow from the US Treasury as trade partners came to fear that the US did not have sufficient gold to meet their dollar claims (it didn't). This ever increasing payout of gold from the US Treasury eventually provoked the so-called "Nixon Shock" of 1971. On that occasion the President of the United States "closed the gold window" of the US Treasury, and by doing so unilaterally brought the Bretton Woods era international gold standard to a sudden end.

Market theorists have a special name for events of this nature. When bankers, government officials, financial writers, and economists invoke the laws of supply and demand to explain how the prices of goods and services rise and fall, they often prefer to leave outside their equations many factors that do not fall within the purview of the standard economic theory.

The many and various phenomena that can affect market prices in general (and the price of gold in particular) are thereby placed in quarantine by mainstream economic thought. This is done by assigning the phenomena in question to the category of "externalities." "Externalities", in economic jargon are those events and forces that can be conveniently regarded as coming from outside the economic system. Two examples will make this clear.

The first and probably most important "externality" that affects world gold markets is the fear of war and the second is war itself. For this reason, one of the most powerful influences on international gold markets is the growth of political and military tensions in the international arena. In his 1987 review of gold markets and gold investment practices, Jeffrey A. Nichols mentioned both the Soviet invasion of Afghanistan as well as to the overthrow of the Shah of Iran and the taking of American hostages (1979) as examples of war and international tension that had caused rapid increases in the price of gold. When the above events occurred almost simultaneously the price of gold leaped from $300 to $800 an ounce.[104]

However, not all increases in world tensions and military activity have the same effect. For example, when the Soviets sent their troops into Afghanistan in December 1979 the gold price remained steady. The Shah of Iran left his country in

---

[104] Nichols, p.43.

January 1979, but the price of gold was not affected. When, however, Iraq invaded Iran in September 1979, the price of gold suddenly shot up. Then, in November of the same year when Muslim fundamentalists in Iran took US embassy personnel hostage, there were exponential increases in the price of gold as all the world watched and waited to see what the United States would do. Later the gold price reached almost $860 in January 1980 before declining again.[105]   Not all examples of war and diplomatic stress of the sort just mentioned have this affect on the price of gold, but those that involve the Middle East and the potential disruption of American oil supplies often do.

One of the things that the 21st Century investor must keep an eye on, therefore, is the fact that after years of warfare, lives and property were still being destroyed in Iraq and Afghanistan in 2010. Consequently, the threat of wider war and the possible cutbacks of petroleum shipments to the United remained in the news. Many things had, however, changed in the international picture by 2010. One of the more interesting changes was the rise of rapidly growing new economies like those of Iran, India, China, and Brazil. All of these countries are now able to bid against the United States for oil, for other raw materials, as well as to compete in industrial markets. In addition to the so-called "externalities" that can affect gold markets, then, there are also powerful influences that arise more

---

[105] *Ibid.*

directly from economic realities, as we shall see in the following final section of the present chapter.

National Debt, Equities, the US Dollar and the Price of Gold

Basic economic forces that can affect the price of gold are as follows:

- the state of equities markets (stocks and bonds) world wide
- the strength of the international reserve currency (US dollar)
- the rate of inflation in the United States (Consumer Price Index)
- the US domestic debt (internal deficits)
- the US foreign debt ($2Trillion to China)
- the US balance of payments (external deficits)
- threat of sovereign defaults (as in Greece in 2010).

In other words, those who wish to protect the value of their savings (cash, equities, real property) should keep their eye not only on the international scene and the reality of war or the threat of war, but on a number of other factors as well. The first of these is the markets for stocks and bonds. Obviously, equities markets represent a broad range of investments with which most investors are familiar most of the time. The usual benchmarks for investing in equities, of course, include price/equity ratios for stocks and bond yields for US Treasury obligations and corporate bonds.[106] Traditionally it has been believed that there is a inverse relationship between these two investment choices. When the stock market is not doing well, the bond market is commonly viewed as a happy place to be and vice versa. This relationship changed after the sharp economic downturn in 2007, however, when, due to the Federal Reserve's program of "easing" (i.e., of lowering interest rates) the return on government bonds hovered around 1%. When, therefore, the prices of corporate shares went into decline while at the same time US Treasury obligations, corporate and municipal bonds are paying off at all time lows, many investors became concerned.

Many investors who were formerly holding primarily stocks and bonds will now begin to consider other types of investment such as buying property or merely placing their wealth in cash while waiting for better times. Many corporations had begun to think the same way by 2010 at which time US corporate entities were reporting cash holdings at far above historic norms. When equities markets become unstable and unproductive, and when corporations hold their wealth in cash, then considering an investment in gold will become more attractive to a very wide range of people. This will be especially true if and when doubts arise about the future of the US dollar. The dollar is still the international reserve currency, and the

---

[106] Price equity ratios compare the stock's current price with the company's underlying value. Bond yields are high when prices are low and vice versa.

United States continues to benefit from this state of affairs. Other countries have to create and to sell goods and services to pay their bills, while the United States has only to create more money. This is done, of course, in the banking sector, but it must be accomplished under the constraints of reserve requirements and inter-bank lending rates set by the US Federal Reserve as explained in Chapter 11 below which describes the role of the Federal Reserve in maintaining the American money supply.

In a situation in which excess liquidity is created by Fed "loosening", rapid inflation becomes a real possibility. This will be especially true as long term domestic and foreign trade deficits begin to form a large (some would say "massive") negative overhang on the US economy. It is in this situation, almost more than any other, that some form of investment in gold will become especially attractive. The US rate of inflation was catastrophically high in several periods towards the end of the 20th Century, for example, with the result that the price of gold left its Bretton Woods levels ($35/oz) for ever. Concerning the US deficits just mentioned, the deficit about which all investors should be concerned is the domestic deficit.

The domestic deficit compares the amount of money spent annually by the Federal Government to the government's tax revenues in that same year. The result of this calculation has been negative for some time. This is a fact which has been the subject of competing Congressional rhetoric by the two American political parties. Historically, the Republicans in

Congress have lamented domestic budget deficits and have presented their party as "fiscally responsible." Historically, the Democrats in Congress have been the ones to argue that "deficit financing" is necessary to keep the economy in good shape and to maintain key social services. Given this history of debate on the House and Senate floor, it is somewhat strange to discover that both parties to the conversation have been in the habit of increasing the public debt year after year.

While the political rhetoric exchanged in Congress concerning the Federal budget don't really matter to the potential investor in gold, the total amount by which the US Government is "in the red" certainly does. When the domestic deficit overhang becomes too large, some people holding significant amounts of US dollars will choose to put some of their money either in stronger currencies, or in gold when there are no reliable currencies to flee to. What is true of the individual investor is also true of the world's central banks. Consequently, the central banks of China, South Korea, Taiwan, and some other Asian nations are currently adding gold to their forex reserves against a possible future weakening of the US dollar such that potential gold investors will also wish to keep this in mind.

In addition to the domestic deficit, of course, there is the international trade deficit. This is created when the United States spends more abroad than it earns from exports to its' foreign trade partners. When this happens what is produced is called a "negative balance of trade." The United States has had a negative balance of trade for some time now. This has been made somewhat easier for the US than it would be for other nations by the fact that the US issues the international reserve currency (the US dollar). The potential gold investor, however, might now be wondering if there is not some sort of natural limit to this state of affairs. One rough estimate of the seriousness of the US negative trade balance is provided by the amount of money that the United States of America owes the Peoples' Republic of China. At present, the US is in debt to China to the tune of more than $2Trillon. The US is also in debt to Japan for a similar amount. These debts are held by America's largest trade partners, largely in the form of US Treasury obligations. When any nation lives on its credit card in this way, it is always possible that there will come a day when that credit card is "maxed out." If and when this happens, many Americans will find that the circumstances of their lives have changed in some unpleasant way. Almost everyone involved, and not the least the Chinese leaders themselves, hopes that such a day will never arrive. If and when it does, however, the prudent investor will already have some sort of a position in gold or will be eager to create one as soon as possible.

Chapter 9 The US Dollar and the Gold/Money Paradox

Pieces of Eight

In the our earlier discussion of commodity money, Virginia's tobacco currency was given as an example of the process by which a commonly produced and generally valuable commodity can quickly make the transition to commodity money, especially when there is no other sort of currency available to do the work of trade. As soon as gold enters the picture to take up this task a paradox presents itself. The gold and money paradox, which will be described in the history of the US dollar that follows, is simply this. Gold is needed to support other forms of money such as bank notes and bank drafts. In times of economic crisis, however, individuals carrying paper "promises to pay" often remove the gold from the bankers' vaults to look after it themselves with the result that, at such times, there is never enough gold to go around.

As noted earlier, Virginia's tobacco money, was relatively quick to develop its paper money *doppelgänger*. The early Virginian tobacco farmers found it convenient to substitute paper notes representing units of tobacco, and not merely because it's easier to do business with paper money. In this case the paper notes were sometimes more valuable than the tobacco that they represented.   The reason was that after the tobacco currency had been in use for some time certain tobacco farmers grew and selected sub-optimal tobacco to play the role of money. The colony, however, eventually built special warehouses and decreed quality codes to curb such abuses and to safeguard the tobacco offered as currency. Suitably regulated in this way, the tobacco currency was used for more than a century in the Chesapeake Bay area.

In 1642 the Virginia legislature made the tobacco currency legal tender (perhaps for the second time) and, at the same time, outlawed contracts requiring payment in gold or silver. In Chapter 5 we saw what young Ben Franklin had to say about this problem in 1729, but for the moment it will be sufficient to say that in Great Britain's North American colonies there was a regular and ongoing shortage of metallic coinage to support the needs of trade. As a result of the shortage of hard cash, the North American British colonists tried in many different ways to create local substitutes for the coin of the realm. The imperial government in London, however, sooner or later, ruled all of these monetary innovations ruled out of court.

Unfortunately, however, after the success of the American revolution and the founding of the Republic the economic problems created by the lack of sufficient amounts of currency to support trade and economic development were not resolved. The same shortage of hard currency that had plagued the business life of the colonists for more than a century continued to make life difficult in the young United States. Worse yet, the shortage of ready cash in metallic form led to a long-lived political conflict in the American body politic over the contentious issues of money and banking. While changing its superficial characteristics from one period to the next, this basic conflict lasted until the creation of the US Federal Reserve bank system in the early years of the 20th Century.

Before 1776, the shortage of specie was exacerbated by the British government's obsession with the mercantilist idea that precious metal (in any and all of its forms) must remain within the mother country, and should not be used for foreign trade except in grave emergencies such as war and/or famine. This mercantilist obsession, quite naturally, led Parliament to pass legislation to forbid sending coins minted in Great Britain to the colonies. In addition to being tight-fisted with the gold and silver coinage, the British rulers also imposed a long list of prohibitions outlawing virtually any kind of monetary initiatives that might be invented by the residents of the colonies to resolve their currency dilemmas. The negative legislation issued in London included laws prohibiting the creation of banks, orders prohibiting the issuance of paper money, and Royal proclamations directing the termination of any colonial attempts to mint their own coinage, operating a mint being a Royal prerogative.

Since minting a coinage, however modest, and providing paper money by operating a bank were equally illegal, one wonders how the masters of the British Empire expected their overseas subjects to do business at all. One answer, as we shall see, is that the rulers of the imperial homeland expected their cash-strapped colonists in North America and the Caribbean to make use of a different currency entirely. This currency, thanks to the adventures of Hernán Cortés and his "conquerors" in Mexico in the previous century, was the universally beloved, marvelously heavy, and widely available Spanish dollar. Colonial governments were quick to respond to this imperial directive. For example, in Virginia, where the tobacco currency had previously been the only form of money with which to conduct business, the colonial population were only too eager to leave one of the more awkward types of commodity money behind and to replace it with metallic currency, even one minted by a different empire. Thus, according to one historian of the dollar, Virginia finally decreed the end of the tobacco currency as the only currency in which debts could be paid (i.e., "legal tender") in 1649 when it directed the residents of the colony to utilize the Spanish dollar in their economic activities.[107]

As already explained, the Spanish coin called the "dollar" was widely used throughout the Americas, and was minted both in Spain and in Spain's American colonies.[108] The Spanish dollar contained 25.56 grams of silver at 0.93055 fine, and was worth eight *reales* in the Spanish coinage.[109] Spanish dollars were, therefore, colloquially referred to as a "pieces of eight" in the phrase so cheerfully croaked out by Long John Silver's parrot in

---

[107] Nussbaum, *op.cit.*, p.
[108] Pond, Shepard, "The Spanish Dollar: The World's Most Famous Silver Coin." *Bulletin of the Business Historical Society*, Vol. 15, No. 1 (Feb., 1941), pp. 12-16,
[109] The word *real* means "royal", and the coin that went by that name was worth about sixpence at the time.

Robert Louis Stevenson's immortal *Treasure Island.* Like the Athenian *Drachma* and the Florentine *Fiorino*, the Spanish dollar was never debased by the Spanish monetary authorities.

As you may have suspected, however, the word "dollar" is not of Spanish origin. Instead, it goes back to the central European (Hapsburg) origins of the Spanish Royal House. When the Hapsburgs were ruling central Europe, assisted by the powerful Fuggers bankers mentioned earlier, a somewhat rebellious local aristocrat by the name of Count Hieronymus Schlick happened to own a silver mine located in the Valley of Joachim in what is today Czechoslovakia. Since the German word for valley is *"tal"*, the coins that were minted in the Count Schlick's mine were dubbed *"Joachimstalers"* after the valley in which they were produced. Before long, however, the syllable "Joachims" dropped off, and the coins, which were used throughout central Europe, were simply called *"talers"* This word soon evolved into the word "dollar", and, thanks again to the very profitable adventures of Hernán Cortés, was uttered in numerous accents throughout the countries of North and South America for centuries. Not only was the sound of the word "dollar" a familiar one in many American countries north and south, but the image that was found on one side of the Spanish coin also gave rise to symbol of the dollar that we use today. This image was a numismatic portrait of two pillars which were meant to symbolize what were then called "the Gates of Hercules." These "gates" stood on either side of the narrow sea lane that separated the Mediterranean sea from the great blue Atlantic world beyond.

It was, therefore, the pillars and the inscribed bunting twining around them on the back of the most widely spent piece of money in the Americas that gave us the dollar sign ($). The widespread use of the Spanish Dollar both within and between the British colonies in North America testified to a shortage of the gold and silver required to carry on an expanding domestic economy as well as to facilitate a constantly growing foreign trade. As noted earlier, the shortage of hard cash that plagued the British colonies had been created by the mercantilist policies of Great Britain. These problems did not, however, disappear, even after the rebellious colonies had made the break with their mother country. Thus, even after the English speaking residents of North America had prevailed over their colonial masters in the American Revolution (1776-1781), the new citizens of the young United States labored under the same shortage of a viable metallic coinage that they had known before. This shortage of "specie" gave rise to a struggle over monetary and banking policy in the United States Congress that lasted more than a century.

The first phase of the long drawn out battle over money and banking that took place in the early national period occupied some of the best minds of the young Republic. Some former subjects of the British King, like Alexander Hamilton, wanted to follow Britain's example, and to found a national bank that would economically empower the young republic by playing the same role that the Bank of England had played in Great Britain since 1694. Hamilton knew that with a national central bank in place it would be possible to provide sufficient "credit" (i.e., paper money) to carry on the business affairs of the newly independent country. Other founders of the nation like Thomas Jefferson, remained suspicious of bankers and clung to their belief that only physical gold and silver could play the role of a national currency.

The monetary fundamentalists who admired Jefferson, therefore, were more than pleased when the first issue of gold and silver coins in the young republic was supervised by Jefferson himself. Theirs would be a hard cash republic! It was largely the farmers and frontiersmen of the youthful United States who looked to Thomas Jefferson for leadership and tended, as he did, to cling to their faith in gold and silver. There was a very good reason for their of bankers and the paper money that bankers are only too happy to issue. Those who had just lived through a revolution had endured a very paradoxical experience with paper money. The American revolution had been financed almost entirely on the basis of paper "promises to pay."

The paper money that the American revolutionaries used had been issued by the Continental Congress, and had worked brilliantly to create the revolutionary army that would confront Britain's imperial might. The paper scrip created by the

Continental Congress put revolutionary soldiers in the field and had worked like magic- but only at first. After its' initial

The Spanish Dollar of 1739 : Can You Spot the Dollar Signs?[110]

successes, the first paper currency issued by the leaders of what would later become the United States experienced a rapid decline in value until it was almost completely worthless. The very same people whom the revolutionary currency had helped

---

[110] Image sourced at:
http://www.google.com/imgres?imgurl=http://www.rba.gov.au/Museum/Displays/
_Images/1788_1900/spanish_dollar_big.jpg&imgrefurl/

to ease themselves out from under the imperial yoke soon forgot how convenient it had been to print money to stage a revolution, and instead came to mistrust money made of paper for the rest of their lives. Please welcome the Continental!

Two Revolutions Financed by Runaway Inflation

When it is considered that the Continental Congress (1774-1776) had no particular power to tax or otherwise to command revenues in the several British colonies which it claimed to represent, it is amazing that the American Revolution took place at all. One scholar who has studied the financial strategy of the Continental Congress in detail has sarcastically referred to certain of the former British colonies as "free riders." This because while they wanted to mount a revolution against the British Crown certain colonies did not particularly want to pay the price for arming the revolutionary citizens and providing for their needs both in battle and in camp. What happened in the storm and stress of the American Revolution that followed was that some of the former colonies (Massachusetts, for example) agreed voluntarily to contribute to the cause and were able to give generously while other colonies were not and did not.[111] We should not perhaps be

---

[111] Baack, Ben, "Forging a Nation State: The Continental Congress and the Financing of the War of American Independence." *The Economic History Review*, New Series, Vol. 54, No. 4 (Nov., 2001), pp. 639-656.

surprised at the reluctance towards revolution shown by some of the colonial leaders.

Surely, given both the expense and the uncertainty of armed confrontation with one of the biggest armies (and the largest navy) in the world, it would not have been shocking had some of the thirteen colonies opted to come to a sensible arrangement with the mother country and to forget all about political revolution. Indeed, as historians of the early days of the American Revolution will tell you, there was a sizeable faction within the Continental Congress that would have been only too willing to come to terms with Great Britain- if only the suddenly irritated and rather violent mother country had been willing to listen.

History, of course, is full of surprises, and the final decision of all the American colonies to meet "kith and kin" on the field of battle in the name of liberty and independence is more surprising than most. On the other hand, war is one of the more expensive pastimes of the human race so that it is equally a cause for wonder and amazement that, somehow, the members of the Continental Congress managed to find the means to recruit and to provision a revolutionary army and to send it into battle. This was the miracle that was accomplished by the Continental Congress. In the process of getting the imperial overlord off their colonial backs, that short lived body provided the world with a financial model for successful revolution upon which both the French Revolution (1791) and the Russian revolution (1917) would later improve. The name of the miracle that the Continental Congress produced is "inflation."

Inflation takes place when increases in the issue of money by the state overtake increases in the production of goods and services in the economy. Only a year after the Declaration of Independence (1776), the amount of money issued by the Continental Congress had increased to two and a half times the amount that had existed before then.[112] In the early stages of the conflict, when a hastily configured Continental Army had to fight professional British troops (which had been increased in number from 7,000 to 27,000 in just one year), the patriotic revolutionaries had good reason to accept the new "Continental" in payment for goods and services. Had they not done so, the loss of their freedom, their property and perhaps even an hangman's rope may have loomed in their futures. Perhaps for this reason and also perhaps because the colonists had already accumulated significant experience with monetary innovation, the Continental Congress' decision to pay for a revolutionary war by simply printing money worked like a charm- but only for a while.

Between 1775 and 1779 there were no less than forty-two currency issues by the Continental Congress.[113] This desperate and profligate production of paper money would, of

---

[112] *Ibid.*, p.642.
[113] Galbraith, *op.cit.*, p.58.

course, lead eventually to runaway inflation, and to the following unhappy phrase that would soon tumble effortlessly from patriotic lips- "Not worth a Continental." The bitter political struggle over the Continental, however, would begin only after the revolution that it had financed had been successful, and the young republic that it had created was attempting to put its monetary house in order. When Alexander Hamilton reminded his fellow citizens, by then seated in the houses of Congress, that the painful process of establishing the credit of the young nation must now begin, many dissented from his view. Hamilton sagely reminded his listeners that honoring all of the bonds issued by the young United States at full value would bring many prominent and well-to-do people to the side of the republic as a manifestation of their own economic interest:

> Those who are most commonly creditors of a nation, are, generally speaking, enlightened men; and there are signal examples to warrant a conclusion, that when   a candid and fair appeal is made to them, they will understand their true interest too well to refuse their concurrence in such modifications of their claims, as any real necessity may demand.[114]

The money that had been advanced by those who had bought the bonds, at whatever proportion of their face value, had not been used in vain. "It was the price of liberty", Hamilton

---

[114] The full text of Hamilton's *Report on Credit* may be conveniently reviewed online at:
http://press-pubs.uchicago.edu/founders/documents/a1_8_2s5.html.

reminded those legislators who did not wish to reward the speculators as well as the patriots. After Hamilton issued this argument in his "Report on Credit", a long, loud, and angry Congressional debate began almost immediately. Somewhat surprisingly, this debate would continue to resound in the houses of Congress, during political campaigns, and across many pages of what was by then a free press throughout the century to follow.

Only a short time later, the French who toppled Louis XVI from his throne had also financed their revolution to overthrow monarchical privilege with paper "promises to pay." Like the Americans before them, the French toppled the power of kings with basically worthless paper money. In France, however, thanks to the emergence of a very effective military dictator, and the great successes registered in his wars of conquest, the French also managed to resolve the problems created by their revolutionary currency, the *assignat*, more quickly than the Americans had been able to do. When the stalwarts of the French revolution had faced problems similar to those that had recently been confronted by the Americans, the French revolutionaries also created a paper currency. In those tense days, France needed an effective currency to finance the wars that were required to keep the reactionary nations of Europe from France's doorstep. While the credit money extravaganza devised by John Law at the beginning of the 18th century no doubt put the idea of a useful paper currency in the minds of the French revolutionaries, they nevertheless hit upon a better idea for backing their paper "promises to pay".

The French *Assignat* differed from the American Continental by virtue of being backed by an economic quantity that could not disappear, namely the soil of France itself. This solution to the problem of revolutionary financing was a far better one than the insurgent British colonists had come up with only a few years before. Eventually, however, the value of the *Assignat* soon declined just as the continental had done. Indeed, to convince the populace that the wartime inflation had, at last, come to an end, the printing presses that had been used to turn out the *Assignat* were publicly smashed in 1792. Not long afterwards, in 1799, the "little corporal", Napoleon Bonaparte, had elected himself as dictator of the French Revolution. Napoleon may have been a political radical, at least for a while, but he was rigidly conservative in almost everything else.[115] Consequently, Napoleon quickly restored a metallic currency to France which, thanks to his many military victories, soon benefited from the financial strength of the European bankers who suddenly found themselves only too willing to finance Napoleon's further efforts on the field of battle.

Meanwhile, in the young republic on the other side of the Atlantic, the problems that had been created by revolutionary

---

[115] An excellent recent portrait of Napoleon and also of the wars needed to discourage foreign powers from restoring the Bourbons is provided by Charles Esdaile in his *Napoleon's Wars: An International History.* New York: Penguin, 2007.

finance continued to trouble a youthful nation. While it might have been expected that monetary problems could be made to disappear from North America after the ordeal of revolutionary war and the creation of a new form of government, this was not what happened. The shortage of ready cash that had plagued the North American colonial economy continued long after the Founders had completed their Constitutional labors in Philadelphia (1787), remounted their horses, and returned to their banks and plantations. The awful shortage of the metallic currency required for trade continued to create economic problems in 19th Century America as the result of the two indomitable economic forces that are next to be explained.

The Dollar War That Lasted A Century

The more important of two forces that led to the shortage of coinage in the early United States was that of the ongoing trade relationship between Great Britain and her former colonies. This meeting of unequal economic forces sucked the metallic coinage out of the youthful United States for many years according to the relentless logic of Gresham's Law. Secondly, the local production of precious metals, and the acquisition of Spanish dollars through the occasional visits of the Caribbean pirates to northern ports, simply could not keep up with the currency needs of a rapidly expanding economy.[116]   The

---

[116] The pirates in question had usually acquired their dollars by attacking Spanish treasure ships in the Caribbean and, hence, were welcomed by the British

shortage of hard cash in the United States lasted until the opening of the western silver mines much later in the 19th century. Then, perversely enough, just as the silver of the western mines finally became available to support the business of the country, the rapidly growing young nation divided itself politically between those who preferred a silver currency and those who preferred gold.

The great division in politics that caused a long and sometimes violent debate over the national currency to continue for many years opposed the middle and far western agricultural and mining partisans of a silver currency to the bankers, traders and industrialists of the eastern and northern states. This latter group generally controlled finance, engaged in international trade, and, charged interest on loans. They, therefore, favored gold as the basis of the national currency both as a creditor class abhorring inflation, and for its more stable relationships with other currencies.[117] Thus, the relative lack of precious metals on the basis of which to create the currency of the newly liberated colonies that had caused Hamilton and Jefferson to disagree was eventually replaced by a struggle between the

---

colonists as fellow Britons who had struck a blow against the national enemy. See Pond, *op. cit.*
[117] Silver was demonetized in the United States in 1873 leading to sharp conflicts between those who favored silver and those who favored gold. See :Friedman, Milton, *Monetary Mischief: Episodes in Monetary History.* New York: Harcourt Brace Jovanovich, 1992. See especially Chapter 4 "The Crime of 1873", pp.51-79.

backers of "free silver" and the more austere (or perhaps merely richer) partisans of a gold based currency.

The legislative struggle that divided the American polity for more than one hundred years had originally begun when dissident voices in Congress opposed the first Secretary of the Treasury, Alexander Hamilton's, recommendation to the effect that the well-heeled speculators who had purchased US government bonds at a discount, should be recompensed at par (i.e., at face value) just as would be those simple patriots who had bought government paper to support the cause of revolution. Hamilton eventually won the support of enough congressmen to achieve his desire that the credit of the young country be soundly established by paying off Federal and state debt instruments at par. Following this, Hamilton devised what turned out to be a very successful system for "funding" the government debt. His position was that holders of government debt would be quite satisfied with regular interest payments whereas Thomas Jefferson also wanted to pay back the principle as well. Hamilton's suggestion was opposed because of its similarity to the highly successful policy first developed by the Bank of England but the first Secretary of the Treasury won out in the end.[118]

---

[118] Swanson, Donald F.,"Thomas Jefferson on Establishing Public Credit: The Debt Plans of a Would-be Secretary of the Treasury?" *Presidential Studies Quarterly*, Vol. 23, No. 3, The Domestic and Foreign Policy Presidencies (Summer, 1993), pp. 499-508. Swanson makes clear that Hamilton's plan which basically proposed paying only the interest on the debt was far

Meanwhile, the shortage of ready cash in the (newly) United States, continued. This came to pass simply because, while the monopoly to create money had been given to the Federal government in the US Constitution, the only type of currency which that document would allow was that of a gold and silver coinage. Banks and banking, which exist, of course, to create paper money, were thereby strongly discouraged. This was the occasion of severe disappointment for Alexander Hamilton who was well aware of the importance of the banker's function for the creation of a new national economy. This somewhat extremist decision to leave the bankers out of the picture by restricting the Federal government to the creation of a metallic coinage was later followed by the struggle between Hamilton and Jefferson over the establishment of the First Bank of the United States.

Before that happened, however, and before Hamilton and Jefferson became political enemies, Jefferson had been kind enough to arrange a compromise between Secretary of the Treasury Hamilton and Hamilton's powerful political rival James Madison over the funding of the national debt. Over dinner in the national capital, which was then New York City, the three founders of the United States made a deal. They agreed that in exchange for Madison's support for Hamilton's policies to

---

superior to Jefferson's which envisaged paying off interest and principal in twenty years. Hamilton's much more effective plan established the credit of the new government, but also began a fateful competition with Jefferson.

resolve the national debt, the Federal capital would moved from busy and commercial New York to the environs of sleepy agricultural Virginia.[119] commercial New York to the environs of sleepy agricultural Virginia.[120] Although Jefferson and Hamilton had worked well together under the first President, George Washington, they would later clash over the role of a central bank in the young republic. The political struggles over money and banking that surrounded the figures of Hamilton and Jefferson were not to be resolved until the creation of the US Federal Reserve system more than one hundred years later.

The next act of the drama over the US dollar featured Andrew Jackson as the champion of farmers and frontiersmen against Nicholas Biddle Director of the Second Bank of the United States. By opposing Biddle's request to renew the charter of the Second Bank of the United States (1836) Jackson was also directly opposing both the financial and business interests of the country. The farmers and frontiersmen led by Andrew Jackson cheered loudly when the short and tumultuous

---

[119] Brands, H.W. in his *The Money Men*. New York: Norton, 2006, pp.47-48 suggests that Thomas Jefferson got Alexander Hamilton and James Madison together over dinner and hammered out a deal. The northerners who wanted assumption of the Federal and state debt at par would get what they wanted while the southerners who wanted a southern capital of the United States got Washington, DC.

[120] Brands, H.W. in his *The Money Men*. New York: Norton, 2006, pp.47-48 suggests that Thomas Jefferson got Alexander Hamilton and James Madison together over dinner and hammered out a deal. The northerners who wanted assumption of the Federal and state debt at par would get what they wanted while the southerners who wanted a southern capital of the United States got Washington, DC.

life of the Second Bank of the United States (1816-1836) came to an end. Their cheers sounded loudly in the halls of Congress of the United States despite the Second Bank's achievements. The Second Bank of the United States, under Biddle's leadership, had been highly effective in handling the debt that had been occasioned by the War of 1812. Notwithstanding this success, and apparently blind the bank's considerable national importance, President Andrew Jackson railed politically against "bankers and speculators", and refused to allow the renewal of the bank's charter.

When the bank's director, Nicholas Biddle, used his extensive financial connections to reign in the creation of bank credit as a way of instructing "Old Hickory" as to what banks were for, the results were severely negative for the conduct of business. One probable result of the struggle between the Jackson White House and Biddel's Second Bank of the United States was to prepare the way for the "panic" of 1837. This economic shutdown brought severe economic hardship not only on bankers in general (many banks failed), but on the lives and fortunes of President Jackson's own political constituency. Nevertheless, Jackson responded to Biddle's slow drainage from the system of what today would be called "commercial paper" by not giving in. Despite the widespread damage to the commerce of the country, Jackson remained intransigent, and eventually Biddle's Second Bank of the United States died an unnatural legislative death.

This was unfortunate since a well-respected national bank would have been very useful for meeting the next national crisis that arose for the United States This would have been the challenge of financing the Federal government's war against the Confederacy during the Civil War (1861-65). What happened instead was an adventure in the government issue of a paper currency that did not always carry a "promise to pay", but which Americans who lived through that tragic and destructive conflict had to use any way. Please welcome the Greenback!

The Greenback Dollar

When a long civil conflict threatened the (previously) United States, and especially after some of the first disasters suffered by the Union Army in the early months of the fighting, the Secretary of the Treasury, Salmon P. Chase, took a look at the books, and announced that the country was nearly broke. The expenditures of the Federal government had risen from $67 Million in 1861 to $475 Million by the end of the following year. As strange as it may seem today, the Federal Government had very little ability to tax the population in those days. Before the arrival of the Income Tax (1913), excise taxes and customs duties provided almost all Federal revenues. President Lincoln attempted to impose an income tax to support the costs of the Civil War, but this proved so unpopular that it was soon withdrawn. Consequently, Federal government revenues were rather low- a mere $67 Million by the end of the second year of the war (1862). Given that Washington had already spent $475 Million to finance that war, the deficit that had been produced was both unprecedented and horrific.[121] Under the circumstances, the Federal government in Washington did exactly what the Continental Congress had done many years before. It simply printed money. The ink used to print the dollars that saved the Union was green, and, thus, the "Greenback" was born. Laboring under the stress of war and realizing that the country would soon be in dire need of loans, Congress quickly made life a little easier for the banking sector in 1861 by suspending the requirement that bank notes would be repaid in specie at the bearer's demand.

When the first $300 Million in Greenbacks were rolled out, therefore, they paid war contractors and Union troops in the same way that the Continental had paid for supplies and soldiers during the American Revolution. A second issue of $150 Million Greenbacks in 1862 carried the notice "Receivable In Payment Of All Public Dues." What this meant was that paper promises to pay were to be accepted by law as "legal tender." This was a direct application of the power of the state to issue the currency. Its' consequence was that, in practice, no one could refuse to accept payment in Greenback dollars for commodities, debts, or taxes. The only bills that had to be settled to the tune of clinking gold coins were customs duties, and the payment of interest on

---

[121] Galbraith, *op.cit.*, p. 92.

the Federal debt. Indeed, it was the customs duties to be collected in shiny gold coin that were intended to pay off those who had invested in the government debt. Like the Continental dollars before them, the Greenbacks did the job they were required to do. In so doing, they not only empowered the Federal government to put an end to the Confederacy by military means, but also allowed "Greenbacks" to remain the official US national currency until 1971 when they were finally replaced by banknotes created by the Federal Reserve which is what you will find in your wallet or purse today.

The Greenback episode did, however, give rise to a near national emergency involving gold. Almost as if they had been listening to the tirades of Jefferson and Jackson earlier in the century, two clever and rapacious market operators, Jay Gould and Jim Fisk, in 1869 almost cornered the New York market in which speculators against the Greenback measured the power of that currency in terms of solid gold dollars. In this particular adventure, Gould and Fisk managed to embody exactly the type of corrupt and disruptive speculative shenanigans that the frontiersman, farmers, and mechanics of the United States had feared since the beginning of the Republic. Only a last minute counter-coup by the recently elected President, U.S. Grant, prevented these New York City financial cutthroats from driving the price of gold (as measured in Greenbacks) through the roof. Had President Grant not moved to sell a fairly large amount of gold held by the US Treasury, and then only just in time, two of the most ruthless speculators known in the rough and tumble world of Manhattan finance would have wrecked the US currency and sent the American economy into still another "panic" and depression.

Gould and Fisk were in the cheap dollar camp. This was the case not only because of their interest in the Erie Railroad, which conveyed American grains to the ports for shipping to European markets, but also because these bandits of New York finance scented the possibility of rapid and massive personal enrichment by means of manipulating the gold/Greenback price. The speculators strategy here was to use Greenbacks buy gold at low prices. This had become possible because the Greenback had strengthened gradually after its Civil War exertions. Gould and Fisk, hoped to buy the largest possible proportion of the gold that was held in New York bank vaults so as to back their trades in the gold market. Getting the largest possible proportion of any commodity traded in markets is called "getting a corner" on those markets, and this is what the two Erie Railroad barons hoped to do. As soon has they had "cornered the market", the two financial bandits would then be in a position to hold the short sellers in the Gold Room for ransom when the price of gold began to rise rather than to fall.[122] Given the proven abilities of these two railroad moguls

---

[122] The speculator who is "short" is betting that the price will fall which will allow him to fill his contract to sell a commodity at a lower price and to thereby pocket the difference between the current and the future price as his profit. Please note

and financial scallywags to stampede the New York financial markets when they took a notion to do so, there was only one massive figure standing in their path. His name was Ulysses Simpson Grant, since 1868 the President of the United States.

Because the government of the United States also had concerns about the health of the Greenback, large amounts of gold were held by the US Treasury to keep the dollar/gold price as stable as possible. This the government would do by buying and/or selling Greenbacks as necessary. Upon taking up his presidential duties, Grant had more than sufficient quantities of gold coins and bullion in the government vaults to allow him to intervene as necessary in the gold/ Greenback market that had blossomed in New York as soon as the Greenback dollar had been issued to the public. Gould and Fisk, who were experts at manipulating this market, also believed that they had achieved a serious degree of influence over the President then sitting in Washington. Thus, the two market manipulators had publicly feted Grant during a river trip on one of their Eire Railroad steam packets. As the champagne flowed freely all the way from New York to Albany, the two conspirators vigorously urged upon the President of the United States the theory that the gold price should be established by market activity and not by government intervention.

---

that as the Greenback slowly recovered, the gold price would be expected fall gradually and, anticipating this, there was a good number of short sellers in the famous "gold room" whom Gould and Fisk hoped to relieve of their ready cash.

Historians of the era now say that Gould and Fisk also felt certain that they had achieved a much less public source of influence over the President and his White House. This Gold and Fisk believed because President Grant's sister-in-law had married a certain Abel Cormin. Mr. Cormin, a casual friend of Gould's, had come under the two speculators influence for a substantial monetary consideration. Corbin could be counted on, Gould and Fisk believed, to urge the President to keep the US government out of the gold/Greenback market.[123]   As it happened, the two conspirator-speculators were wrong. After several weeks of wild speculative activity in the Gold Room the gold/Dollar price had motored up from a range of 35-42 Greenbacks over par, to 62 Greenbacks over par. This meant that every gold dollar in your possession would get you 62 Greenbacks. By the time this happened the "shorts" were already running scared.

To deepen the mystery, Gould and Fisk had separated the tasks of manipulating the passions of the "Gold Room." Fisk had been buying gold ostentatiously, and because of his buoyant personality and evil reputation, had been the major source of pressure for inflating the golden bubble and thus eviscerating the trembling short players. Gould, meanwhile, had come to suspect that President Grant would not remain aloof from the chaos in the Gold Room, and had begun quietly to sell his

---

[123] The story of the near corner of the gold market is best told by H.W.Brands, *Op.Cit.*, pp138-158.

position enjoying as he did so gold prices that were far higher than before. Then, to everyone's great surprise, President Grant did indeed intervene. His agents in New York sold all the gold required to deflate the bubble at any price asked and the gold price collapsed overnight. At the end of the affair Gould, who had already sold his gold at the higher prices, was much richer than before.   Fisk did not mourn his fate as a newly impoverished speculator for long, however, since he died at the hands of a rival lover on the principal staircase of a New York hotel shortly afterwards. Gould and Fisk's gold caper brought what was probably the most outrageous partnership of 19th Century New York financial markets to an untimely end. It did not, however, bring the unfortunate Greenback any relief.

Consequently, the third character in the story of Gould and Fisk's attempted gold corner, namely gold itself, continued to roil financial markets in the United States through the end of the 19th century. Serious economic downturns occurred in 1873, in 1893, and again in the very serious depression year of 1907. During these catastrophic events not only the Greenback, but also the whole American economy required rescue. This was accomplished by the largesse of New York's most powerful banker, J.P. Morgan, who, on no less than two occasions, provided funds in solid gold coin to the US Government in a successful effort to support the Greenback dollar. The "panic of 1907" was the last financial upheaval and economic crash in the United States before the creation of the Federal Reserve system in 1913. By that time, however, gold had been both the villain and the savior of the late 19th and early 20th Century American economy a number of times.

Buying gold today, of course, is not the wild and unpredictable adventure that it was in the Gould and Fisk era as you will learn in the following chapter. Chapter 10 is devoted to the necessary details concerning the several ways to hold gold now available to you, and it will also describe in some detail how to operate in these markets.

Chapter 10 Buying Gold: Strategies and Terms

Three Major Types of Gold Investment

We have covered the history of money systems going all the way back to the ancient Babylonians. What this history shows is that, as trading economies developed, the inconvenient commodity monies like oxen (Homer) and *shekels* of barley (ancient Babylon) were eventually replaced by the use of the precious metals gold and silver. The reason for this was, of course, that precious metals were more portable, divisible, and durable than he many other items used as commodity money. Then, very early in the history of money, the invention of banking put the precious metals in the vaults of the bankers who then provided pieces of paper representing the gold or silver coins in their vaults these being rather too heavy to carry around and much too tempting to robbers and thieves. This was all very convenient, of course, and the system worked quite well when business was good.

Business, however, was not always good. In times of economic crisis, large numbers of people tended to show up at the bank to claim their silver and gold. This action made those who did so feel more secure, but at the same time made the paper currency in place less secure. The removal of gold and /or silver from the bankers' vaults caused any number of currency crises in many countries and at many points in time. It also inhibited economic recovery in almost every case. On some occasions, however, as, for example, when war and revolution came along, paper currencies were created by the countries involved. Two examples of revolutionary currencies were the continental in North America and the *assignat* in France. These were paper currencies that were accepted under unusual conditions and on the good faith assumption that they would eventually be redeemed. So far so good.

The monetary problems that the world is dealing with today, however, began when the essential link between the commodity basis of money and the power of the government to issue a national currency was broken. When there is no commodity money to anchor the monetary creations of the state, there is often trouble in store. As we will see in the chapter that follows, Richard Nixon broke the link between the US dollar and gold in 1971. This action brought to an end the Bretton Woods system that had made international trade possible since the end of the Second World War. But not for long. Soon after the "Nixon Shock", the President and his Secretary of State, Henry Kissinger, talked the rulers of Saudi Arabia into the practice of accepting only US dollars in exchange for their oil. The result of this arrangement was that the dollar had a commodity backing (petroleum) once again, and, as such, continued to play the role of international reserve currency right down to recent times.

The question the world is facing at the end of the first decade of the 21st Century, therefore, is just how long the dollar will be able to play this role. If the US government deficits created by attempts to stimulate the economy become too large, if the costs of war become too great to bear, if the US balance of trade stays too negative for too long, and/or if world political tensions increase to the detriment of international trade, then the long reign of the US dollar could come to an end. The massive domestic deficits, the immense foreign debt, and the immense costs of imposing and implementing the *Pax Americana* could vastly weaken the US currency. If and when this happens, everyone holding US dollars, from multi-billionaires like George Soros to ordinary people whose retirement portfolios are full of dollar-denominated securities will be facing incredible losses. There are several ways to offset those losses, but the best and quickest way may be to buy gold. There are three main ways to do this. Here they are in capsule form:

Gold Physicals (long term investment, low risk)

- gold coins (mint editions, collectors editions and heritage coins)
- gold bars (for personal and/or vault storage)

Gold Related Investments (medium term investment, medium risk)

- gold mining stock
- exchange traded funds (ETFs)

Gold Futures Markets (short term speculation, high risk)

- margins and coverage
- buy one / hold one strategy
- pyramiding up
- roll over costs
- open interest
- commitment of traders
- warehouse stocks

We will now take a brief look at how, in practical terms, you can buy gold. At the same time we will consider some of the economic variables that you will want to keep your eye on depending on which form of gold ownership you choose. A special caveat is in order in each case. While holding gold physicals has a small risk coefficient, there are storage costs, insurance, and sales taxes to be paid. While buying gold mining stocks seems perhaps an easier way to go, mining companies wildly differ in terms of the security of their earnings and dividends, so the potential investor must perform the same careful research he or she would do when buying any other equities. Finally, for those who don't mind the risk and who would also like to turn a profit while protecting their wealth against inflation, speculation in gold in the commodities futures market presents a tempting alternative.

A warning must be entered in this last case. When we are talking about speculation in the gold futures market, it must be remembered that the level of risk in commodities futures markets is extremely high. What this means that the small investor (and even some of the big ones) can lose their entire investment within minutes, so be warned! Now let's look at the three ways to buy gold a little more closely.

Holding Physical Gold

As noted earlier, each of the three ways to hold gold have a different level of risk. Holding physicals has the lowest risk of the three. If you acquire gold bullion coins or gold bars, you will always have the gold itself as insurance and you would lose value if it fell below the purchase level. This can certainly happen, but if we look at the last thirty-five years of gold prices, gold unsurprisingly in tandem with almost all other commodities, has never fallen back to the lows that it touched towards the end of the 1970s. However, the price of gold has increased rapidly since the year 2002.[124] The markets for gold coins and gold bars have changed somewhat over the past twenty years.[125] What has changed things in recent times, however, is that the widespread use of the Internet now makes it possible to purchase gold coins and gold bars without leaving your home, and, in some cases, without paying a sales tax. As always, however, there is still the basic difference between the numismatic value (let's call it "collector value") and the gold value of the coins that you buy (let's call it "bullion value"). Most investors in physical gold are not really interested in the numismatic or "collector value" of the coin but only in its gold content or "bullion value." What is important to notice in this case is that some of the very popular gold coins issued by the national mints are of 22 karat quality which is .9167 pure gold. These are coins like the US Gold Eagle and the South African Krugerrand. These coins have a small base metal content to prevent the loss of precious metal through wear. Other coins, such as the Canadian Maple Leaf, however, are made of 24 karat gold (999.999 pure). So don't carry these around in your pocket!

While it is still possible to purchase gold coins from major banks and local coin stores, it is now equally possible to

---

[124] For historical charts of gold prices go to kitco.com. You will find a chart covering the years from 1975 to the present at:
http://www.kitco.com/charts/livegold.html.
[125] When Jeffrey Nichols, wrote his guide to buying gold in 1987 there was no Internet and hence no Internet sales. See Nichols pp. 91-112.

use retail coin sellers who post their offerings on the Internet. When buying locally, of course, you may be paying a sales tax which will add to the cost of your investment. Whether dealing with a local coin store or an Internet coin merchant, however, it is important to make sure you are buying from a reputable dealer who has been in business a reasonable length of time. In this case, there is a difference between what you will pay for the coin (**"asked"**) and what dealers will offer when you want to sell the coin (**"bid"**). The difference between the "bid" and "asked" is called **"the spread"**, and of course it is to your advantage that the "spread" be as small as possible. Depending on which coin you decide to buy, there is also a premium over the spot price of gold that obtains at the time you place your order. Since these premiums vary considerably from retailer to retailer, and from coin to coin, it is important to shop around.

The main costs encountered in holding physical gold are the sales tax and storage costs and insurance. The storage costs range from small (a safety deposit box) to the slightly higher fees charged for secure storage facilities. These fees will go up as the gold price increases as they are usually applied as some percentage of that price. If you store your gold at the bank it is important to know if you are paying for **"allocated storage"** or if your gold is **"commingled"** with that owned by other people. This is important because, if and when a bank fails and there are creditors at the door, the allocated storage option will protect your investment more effectively.

Gold Mining Shares and Exchange Traded Funds

Buying gold mining shares carries about the same amount of risk as investing in any other corporate shares but this may be an asset class that is not correlated to standard indices such as the S &P. Non-correlation with equities may be highly desirable in terms of portfolio allocation and risk diversification. There are large gold companies and small ones. There are those that always manage to be profitable and those that sometimes have a hard time of it. Gold companies range from those with well-developed profitable mines to "juniors" who have no earnings at all and little more than some claims for which they must raise equity in order to explore and develop. Some gold mining companies are located in countries where the stockholder is well protected by the laws(e.g. Canada), whereas others are located in countries where civil government and the laws are not overly protective of the stockholder. A good place to compare gold mining companies is on a website called "mingingnerds.com." This website, despite its' whimsical title, provides extensive information on mining companies and also extensive daily news coverage on market developments in precious metals in general and on gold prices in particular. Miningnerds.com provides the visitor with information on gold mining companies, and also on the production and sales of other precious metals such as silver, platinum, and palladium.[126] The site has an entire page devoted to a long list of gold mining companies that are "listed in all countries." This refers to with an Inc. or a PLC. after their names. Some large international mining companies that mine gold in addition to many other minerals are not, however, to be found on the miningnerds.com list. Another good source of information is the Canadian weekly "The Northern Miner" which has detailed news on the Canadian "junior" miners, usually penny stocks, who are raising funds for exploration and development.

One example of a large company would be Australia's BHP Billington. BHP Billington is the largest mining company in the world followed closely by Rio Tinto mines. In addition to gold and other precious metals, BHP Billington mines iron ore, manganese, petroleum, and aluminum ore (bauxite) an many other minerals.[127] If you are primarily interested in gold mining shares, therefore, you will not be so very interested in acquiring shares in this company. The reason for this is that gold bearing minerals make up only a small part of BHP's output of metallic ores. What this means is that BHP shares will tend not to reflect either the rises or the declines in the international spot price for gold. In other words, unlike the shares of industrial, commercial, and banking corporations, the shares that you may

---

[126] Available online at: http://miningnerds.com/
[127]"BHP Billiton", Wikipedia. Available online at:
http://en.wikipedia.org/wiki/BHP_Billiton#Operations.

buy in gold mining companies will be relatively more productive when the gold price is rising. What follows from this is that the time to buy shares in gold mining companies is when gold prices are increasing and when, for this reason, the value of your gold mining company shares is also increasing. Conversely, gold mining shares will be relatively less profitable when the gold price holds steady or goes into decline. If you are a typical medium-term gold investor concerned merely to balance your portfolio with some gold related equities, you would probably want to consider selling your gold mining company shares as gold prices go into decline.

Now let's take a look at Canada's Barrick Gold, PLC, to see how this works out in practice. As noted earlier, Barrick's CEO, Aaron Regent, recently told interested investors in London that a "Hubbert's Peak" for gold mining may already have been reached. Nevertheless, in the era of rising gold prices Barrick Gold's profits (and its share price) rose rapidly. At a stockholders meeting in Canada in 2010, Barrick's Chairman, Peter Munk, pointed to one of the powerful forces in international markets that was just then forcing up the price of gold: "Every day a new crisis occurs" Munk told his stockholders, "another layer of people think 'I have to protect my wealth.'"[128]

---

[128] Dvorak, Fred and Welsh, Edward, "Barrick's Profit Soars on Gold Pricing: Canadian Miner Benefits as Metal Nears Record and Production Expenses are Held in Check", *The Wall Street Journal*, April 29, 2010, p. B8.

The "crisis" that Barrick CEO Peter Munk was talking about was the possibility of sovereign debt default. Sovereign debt default occurs when a countries like Greece (2010), Argentina (2002), and the Russian Federation (1997,) finally have to admit that they cannot pay back their loans. When this happens, bankers all over the world suddenly can't sleep at night and the gold price inexorably rises. In addition to sovereign default, there is also the very real possibility pointed out by Barrick Gold's CEO that the "Hubbert's peak" for gold mining has already been passed. Some of the production figures released by Barrick Gold at their 2010 meeting also revealed some very interesting facts about what is going on in the world wide gold mining scene. One revealing symptom of the increasing difficulty of getting gold out of the ground was the incredible differences that could be observed between the costs of producing an ounce of gold in Barrick's different mining locations around the world. For example, in 2010 Barrick Gold reported world wide average "total cash costs" of mining an ounce of gold at $466/oz. At the same time, the total cash cost price of mining the gold found at its Lagunas Norte mine in Peru came in at $148/oz.[129] What these highly variable figures may show is that as long as new mines opening up have a high quality ore to process, the profits of mining companies will be maintained, especially in the context of a constantly increasing

---

[129] Barrick Gold online at: http://barrick.com/Home/default.aspx.

gold price. As Barrick Gold's report on the costs per ounce recorded for its 26 mining operations spread all over the world, there are no other mines with costs as low as the Lagunas Norte mine in Peru. Barrick is one of the world's lowest cost producers. This means that as the price of gold increases, Barrick's profits will rise less percentage-wise than those of a high-cost producer whose costs, for instance, are $700-800 per ounce.

Thus, while it was revealed at the May April 28, 2010 stock holders meeting that Barrick Gold had "trimmed" its administrative staff and lowered costs even as gold prices were rising, it was also reported that mine production had been halted by court action at Barrick Gold's potentially rich Cortez mine in Nevada. The Nevada court told Barrick to stop mining in Nevada in response to court actions brought by Native American groups in that state who opposed the violation of their sacred lands and the destruction of the environment that gold mining usually brings about. This is still another point that potential investors in gold mining stocks will have to bear in mind. When we contrast the examples of mining gold in Peru and Nevada, it seems clear that both political and environmental considerations can pose major constraints to gold mining activity. However, investors will naturally see the political climate in Nevada or the US as much more stable than that of Peru, with the threat of nationalizations or unexpected state levies. Hence, investors will normally value mining assets in stable countries at a higher level than those in less stable countries.

Open pit gold mining destroys the landscape while the use of cyanide leaching techniques to retrieve gold from tons and tons of gold bearing soils can seriously pollute regional water tables. All of this to the contrary and notwithstanding, Barrick Gold has done extremely well in the recent period of rising gold prices. However, as just pointed out, investors will want to keep an eye both on the share price and on the dividends paid by Barrick Gold if and when gold prices begin to decline. As a final point, it may be worth repeating that if, indeed, the "Hubberts peak" for gold has already been passed, then the constantly diminishing amounts of more and more expensive gold brought to market will push gold prices relentlessly upwards.

Finally, the medium-term gold investor may also wish to look into a relatively new investment option known as "exchange traded funds" or ETFs. In general, ETFs are only about ten years old. If you were to buy share(s) in an ETF for gold, you would usually (not always!) be buying an actual quantity of physical gold that the ETF is holding in a secure location. In most cases the ETFs dealing in gold demand a minimum purchase of one Troy ounce of gold. One extremely important point to notice here is that while most ETFs selling shares in gold have physical gold deposits in their warehouses, there are some ETFs that do not. Therefore, before buying ETF shares you will want to know if the ETF that you are dealing with holds actual physical gold.

Since most ETFs do, in fact, possess actual physical gold, they now represent a small but significant part of world demand for this precious metal. Thus, ETFs now hold some 1,750 tonnes of gold in secure storage facilities.[130] What the ETFs are offering the investor, then, is the convenience and security of owning "paper gold." There are, however, some storage fees to be paid. In addition, there are the inevitable capital gains taxes that investors must pay if and when there is a a profit on their "paper gold." In the United States this will be the usual capital gains tax which (through 2010) can range from 10% to 35% depending on the income tax rate you are assessed for.[131]

Commodity Futures Markets for Gold Investors

The basic dynamics of commodity futures markets were explained in Chapter 8. It will be useful here, however, to recall the terminology used in these markets in a brief glossary of key terms:

- **futures contract**- a contract to buy or sell a certain quantity of gold at a given price on a specified future date

---

[130] "Exchange Traded Funds", Wikipedia. The first ETF for gold began operations in Australia in 2003. Online at: http://en.wikipedia.org/wiki/Gold_exchange-traded_fund

[131] Capital gains are now assessed at a progressive tax rate. See "Capital gains tax in the United States", Wikipedia. Online at:
http://en.wikipedia.org/wiki/Capital_gains_tax_in_the_United_States

- **long-** a contract to <u>buy</u> a certain quantity of gold at a given price on a specified future date (assumes price rise)
- **short-** a contract to <u>sell</u> a certain quantity of gold at a given price on a specified future date (assumes price fall)
- **hedgers-** producers and consumers of gold who sell and buy actual physical gold
- **speculators-** those who buy and sell futures contracts for financial gain, and who usually "close out" their contracts before the delivery date and sometimes even before the end of the trading day
- **commodity exchanges-** markets where commodity futures contracts are bought and sold such as the COMEX in New York and the CBOT in Chicago

The commodities futures market in gold is used by the hedgers to establish the prices they will receive or will pay, respectively, in the course of everyday business operations. The speculators, on the other hand, are in commodities futures markets only to make a profit. In the course of doing this, however, speculators accomplish three very useful things: 1) they help to determine appropriate prices for commodities by making considered judgments concerning supply and demand for the commodity being traded; 2) they accept the risk of rising and/or falling prices in gold markets which is thereby transferred from the producers and consumers of gold to speculators; and finally, 3) they also provide "liquidity", meaning that participants can enter and leave these markets easily because there will always be many potential buyers or sellers on the other side of the trade. One of the best ways to understand what happens in the commodity futures market for gold is to take a look at the information that the largest commodity exchange for gold futures, the COMEX in New York, publishes every day. We will begin with a COMEX chart ending May 14, 2010.[132]

- The closing day is indicated on the top left (May 14, 2010).
- The closing price for the week follows ($1227.4)
- The green type indicates that the market closed up $17.42 on the week, a number in red would indicate the contrary
- The closing day is indicated on the top left (May 14, 2010).
- The closing price for the week follows ($1227.4)
- The green type indicates that the market closed up $17.42 on the week, a number in red would indicate the contrary
- The entries O, H, and L are for the opening, high, and low for the week
- The chart below is a bar chart each bar showing the high and low for the day over the last two years or so
- On the lower left, Volume (bar chart) shows the total number of trades for the week
- Also on the lower left, Open Interest (red line) shows how many contracts were still open at the end of the week; the number (in red) is the total open interest as of May 14, 2010
- The initials RSI stand for "relative strength index" which is a tool of technical analysis[133]

[132] The COMEX website is online at: http://futures.tradingcharts.com/chart/GD/W
[133] As mentioned earlier, technical analysis of prices in commodities markets is a very popular and very contentious subject, and is not recommended for readers of this book. The basic definition of RSI is as follows: "The Relative Strength Index (RSI) is a trading indicator in the technical analysis of financial markets. It is

09/03/2010 C=1249.2   O=1237.1 H=1251.5 L=1237.1 Mov Avg 3 lines

RSI 60.68 20.00 80.00

Volume 441613.00 Open Interest 574764.00

O   2009   A   J   O   2010   A   J

Created with SuperCharts by Omega Research

You may choose a "full service" broker or a "discount broker." Whichever one you choose, however, the rules and contract specifications of the COMEX, the main futures market for gold, are given in the following list.

Contract Specifications:GC,COMEX

---

intended to indicate the current and historical strength or weakness of a market based on the closing prices of completed trading periods. It assumes that prices close higher in strong market periods, and lower in weaker periods and computes this as a ratio of the number of incrementally higher closes to the incrementally lower closes." For the full discussion see "Relative Strength Indicator", *Wikipedia*. Online at: http://en.wikipedia.org/wiki/Relative_Strength_Index

Trading Unit: 100 troy ounces

Tick Size: $.10/oz. = $10.00

Quoted Units: US $ per troy ounce

Initial Margin: $4,300 **Maintenance Margin:** $3,250

Contract Months: All 12 months.

First Notice Day: Last business day of month preceding contract month.

Last Trading Day: Third last business day of the month.

Trading Hours: Open outcry trading is conducted from 8:20 A.M. until 1:30 P.M. Electronic: 3:15 P.M. on Mondays through Thursdays and concluding at 8:00 A.M. the following day. Sundays, the session begins at 7:00 P.M. All times are New York time.

Daily Limit: $75.00 per ounce

Trading on the COMEX[134]

The standard contract on the COMEX is for 100 troy ounces of gold. Prices are quoted in US dollars per troy ounce. The **initial margin** is the amount of money that you must deposit with your broker to control (i.e. "buy" or "sell") one contract of gold. On the day reported in the graph shown earlier,

---

[134] Online at: http://futures.tradingcharts.com/chart/GD/W

this would amount to about three and one half percent of the total value of the contract. The **maintenance margin** is the minimum amount that you must have in the account in order to maintain the position. Your account is "marked to market" in real time. Should your account fall below the maintenance margin level, then you would get a **margin call** from your broker who would ask you to send him more money to bring it back to the initial margin level or else the position will be liquidated.

The COMEX trades gold futures contracts all year long. The **first notice day** reminds those holding contracts that these contracts must be "closed out" (i.e., either bought or sold) within the next month. The **last trading day** rule reminds you that you may not "close" a contract in the last three working days of the month. Finally, the **daily limit** notice informs those trading gold futures on the COMEX that the maximum one-day increase or decrease in the price of gold is $75 per ounce. The commodity trader's jargon term for such events is to say that the market is locked **"limit down"** on those occasions when the price has dropped $75 from the previous day's close, and to say that the market locked **"limit up"** when the opposite is true. Gold can trade limit up or limit down if there are willing buyers or sellers at that level, and it can come off those levels too. These are the basic rules, schedules, and specialized terms that apply on the COMEX in New York City. The basic advantages and disadvantages of trading commodity futures contracts in gold there and elsewhere are as follows. Many investors sitting on one or more futures contracts in gold will want to **"roll over"** their contracts before they expire. The "longs", of course, are hoping that the gold price will rise while the "shorts" are hoping that it will fall. To do this, speculators will simply close out their nearby position and establish a similar position in a more distant month.

Commodity Futures Markets for Gold Investors: A Warning!

To begin with you should be aware that <u>most people who play commodities markets lose</u>, so be warned! That being said, for day-to-day trading in commodity futures markets the speculator has several strategic and tactical and factors to keep in mind. Let's start with strategy:

- margins and coverage
- stop loss orders
- roll over costs
- open interest
- commitment of traders
- warehouse stocks

These are the strategic factors to watch.

The tactical considerations for trading commodity futures in gold include:

- pyramiding
- taking delivery

The initial margin and maintenance margin for commodities futures contracts were mentioned earlier. The

initial margin is what you must pay to control one contract and the **maintenance margin** is the minimum amount that you must keep in your account. For the COMEX in New York, for example, these margins are $4,300 (initial) and $3,250 (maintenance). In other words, when the gold price hit $1200/oz in May 2010, you were controlling $120,000 worth of gold for a minimum investment of $4,300. At this point you were leveraged at almost 25:1. That of course would be foolhardy, as you would get a "**margin call**" if you lost $1,050, in other words if gold dropped $10.50 per ounce at any time from your initiation of the long position, not at all a big daily move for gold. However, if one opened the account with $10,000 and went long or short one contract, it would take a drop of $6,750 or $67.50 per ounce in order to trigger a margin call. Prudent futures speculators, if that is not an oxymoron, will often have at least double and sometimes 3 to 4 times the initial margin level in their accounts. Even at these levels, there is significant leverage. During, for example, the 1980s the gold price could move four or five dollars a day and investors had plenty of time to make up their mind about holding on to their contract (s) or selling out. By 2010, however, daily movements of fifteen and twenty dollars a day were not uncommon. In markets like these the smaller player can be wiped out fairly quickly, so, once again, be warned!

The best way to prevent big losses is to decide just how much you can afford to lose and then to put in a "**stop loss** order" or, colloquially, a "stop." The stop loss order is communicated to your commodities broker by telephone or, in more recent times, by your computer. This is an order that you place telling your commodities broker to sell your contracts if /when the price of gold falls to a certain level. It is recommended by most experienced traders that you should make up your mind in advance about how much you are prepared to lose on your market play and enter either a real or a mental "stop loss" for that price. A stop loss will not guarantee your order will be filled at the indicated price. Once it reaches that level, the order becomes a "market" order and it is filled at the prevailing market price, which, in a fast market, could be worse than the stop price.

It is, of course, important for you to know what the other participants in the gold futures market are doing. Consequently, it will be very important to keep an eye on the figures that give you the "**open interest**" and the "**commitment of traders.**" The former is the number of contracts that are "open" at the end of the day in other words, contracts that remain outstanding and have not been closed out by an offsetting buy or sell order. This is shown at the bottom of the COMEX chart given earlier. The open interest figure can give you a rough estimate or "gut feeling" about the level of interest in gold markets. In periods of small price movements this figure is liable to be lower while in periods of larger movements this figure will usually be higher. The Commitment of Traders report is made available by the

Commodity Futures Trading Commission (CFTC) on Friday each week, and this report will tell you the composition of traders holding long positions and short positions and, as for larger traders who have to report their holdings weekly, the number of large long and short traders in gold.[135] This figure will allow you to assess the views of the market by hedgers, large speculators (often hedge funds) and the remaining non-reporters (who are usually the public; remember these are usually also the losers).

The final three points listed above have to do with your tactical decisions as a speculator in the futures market in gold. A bolder approach to the same problem is called **"pyramiding ."** All this means is that you use your profits to buy additional contracts. Such an approach would have been very profitable for investors (who had adequate margins) during the past ten year period. The so-called "pyramiding" strategy is a strategy that has been used in the past to great advantage by very careful and disciplined speculators in commodities and currencies markets. The upside of the "pyramiding" strategy is that in constantly rising markets it is possible to make large amounts of money. However, few if any markets are "constantly rising."

The dangerous downside of the pyramiding approach is that the newcomer to commodities speculation who enjoys the feelings of sudden unearned wealth can undergo dangerous psychological changes. Since he or she has "won" so far, there is

---

[135] Available online at: http://www.cftc.gov/

a natural tendency for individuals to feel that their knowledge of markets and even their IQ has been increasing along with the price of gold. This may generate a feeling of economic invulnerability that can make it very difficult to "sell out" when the market turns against the investor- as it will! To fail to "lock in" profit while holding out for even greater gains (sometimes called "greed") is the most typical cause of failure in the gold futures market. It is probably also the main reason that most speculators lose when they "play" commodities. So, for the third time, be warned!

There is a final tactical option for the gold futures gold speculator and to consider this option we return to the world of the investor who is primarily in gold markets to protect his or her wealth or to achieve speculative gains. This option is called **"taking delivery."** When you hold futures contracts in gold, it is always possible to do what you have "promised" to do when you took a long position in gold futures. This is to buy the gold when the contract comes due. At current prices, of course, this could amount to a lot of money. Had you decided to do so in May 2010 when the gold price reached $1200/oz., for example, you would have had to pay $120,000.00 to clear your contract for 100 ounces of gold on the Comex. For those who have a large amount of wealth to protect, on the other hand, this would not pose a major problem. It would also convey important advantages. These are the same advantages that accrue to those who hold other forms of "paper gold." If you had been prepared simply to **"take delivery"** on your gold futures contract on the abovementioned date, you would be issued a warehouse certificate entitling you to delivery of one hundred ounces of gold held in an exchange-approved COMEX warehouse. There would be no gold brokers' commission fees to pay, no need to have your 100 ounces of gold assayed, and no concerns about its secured location and no sales tax! There would only be an annual storage fee to be met and, of course, the capital gains tax on any profits you had achieved. Our brief look at the several buying strategies open to the speculator in gold futures markets may be ended here.

The foregoing has been intended as only the most schematic guide to the three basic forms of investment in gold. Long term gold investment in gold bullion coins or in the "paper gold" offered by ETFs holding physical gold are relatively conservative options. Medium term investment in gold mining shares bears roughly the same amount of risk as buying shares in any corporation. Speculation in gold commodity futures, on the other hand, is the most risky investment of the three discussed here, albeit one which holds out a higher potential profit. Any reader of this book who wants to opt for this third possibility of gold investment in futures markets is strongly recommended to look into the matter in much greater detail before taking the plunge. Will it really become necessary to do any of this? All the signs seem to be pointing to a yes answer here, however the final historical survey of gold and money offered in the following final chapter may help to clear up the matter for you should you seriously begin to consider protecting your savings (or to turn a profit) by buying gold.

Chapter 11 The US Dollar: Then and Now

The Gold/Money Paradox

The American dollar had a savior during the two episodes of economic slowdown and financial "panic" that occurred at the very end of the 19th Century and at the very beginning of the 20th. What both the crises of 1893 and 1907 provide, therefore, are good illustrations of the basic gold/money paradox described in Chapter 9. This paradox consists in the fact that that while commodity money in general and gold in particular have provided the necessary support for paper currencies throughout much of human economic history, there has rarely been enough gold available in any given economy to play this role when economic disaster arrives as it always does. As the following will show, President Grant's decision to provide gold to save the Greenback in Jay Gould and Jim Fisk's attempt to corner the New York gold market just following the Civil War was not the last time that a sudden infusion of gold coin was required to save the US dollar.

How J.P. Morgan Saved the Dollar- Twice

One of the more exciting moments of the "panic of 1893" occurred when New York City's financial giant, J.P. Morgan (1837-1913) had an uninvited interview with US President Grover Cleveland. Morgan simply took the train to Washington (he traveled in his private car, of course), and took a room in a Washington hotel. He then announced that he would remain there until the President of the United States chose to see him. More than twenty years of America's bi-metallic currency and its associated problems had prompted the last great robber baron's portentous Washington, DC journey.[136]

One of the stranger outcomes of the "panic of 1873", just twenty years before Morgan's visit to Washington, had been a piece of Congressional legislation that had quietly nudged the United States onto the gold standard. This may have made a lot of sense at the time because it helped to bring the infamous "Greenback era" of marked inflation and economic instability to an end.[137] On the other hand the war between those Americans who loved silver and those who loved gold continued. The 1873 Coinage Act quietly left silver out of the monetary equation for the first time since the US Constitution (1787) had specified that

---

[136] Brands, H.W., *The Money Men: Capitalism, Democracy, and the Hundred Years War Over the American Dollar*. New York: Norton, 2006. On Morgan's actions to save the dollar see especially pp.175-179.

[137] Friedman, Milton, *Monetary Mischief:Episodes in Monetary History*. New York: Harcourt Brace Jovanovich, 1992. On the Coinage Act of 1873see especially pp.51-79.

the money supply of the United States was to consist of gold and silver coins.

The 1873 act, sometimes called "the crime of '73", put the score between the two sides in the lengthy political war over the US dollar at about 100:1 in favor of eastern bankers (who favored gold), and against western farmers and miners (who favored silver). The 1873 Coinage Act was, therefore, a potentially troublesome piece of legislation, especially since silver was, just then, being produced in larger and larger quantities thanks to mining discoveries in the western states. The 1873 Coinage Act simply directed the US treasury to buy gold and made no mention of silver. This was an omission that caused the advocates of "free silver" to go on the warpath. Citizens who wanted a silver-backed currency began the political struggle to re-establish silver as a monetary metal in the United States. This class of Americans, especially the farmers, tended to need cheap credit. They believed that "free silver" (meaning that any amount of silver could be brought to the US Mint for coinage) would provide what they needed. Thus, farmers believed that silver money would give them cheaper bank loans, while the silver miners were eager to secure a Federal buyer for their output. Both parties also tended to believe that bank credit would be generally much tighter under a gold standard regime simply because, as prior experience had taught them, there is never really enough gold to go around.

When the farming and mining populations counter-attacked the eastern bankers

in the halls of Congress they managed to even the score. Five years later (1878) the Bland-Allison Act was passed. This law simply directed the Treasury of the United States to buy silver on a more or less continuous basis. Legally, this made sense, of course, since the Constitution of the United States still directed that the country's economy and money supply should be based on a metallic currency comprised of both gold and silver coins.[138] Politically, however, the Bland-Allison Act merely raised the stakes in the ongoing conflict over the metallic basis of the national currency between those who wanted silver and those who preferred gold. No small part of the energy powering the political battle was provided by the fact that the ratio of silver to gold was changing all the time as silver became cheaper and cheaper, thanks to the back breaking toil of the silver miners.

At the US Mint, the official ratio of silver to gold had originally been set at 16:1. The market price of silver, on the other hand, had declined constantly through the later 19th Century thanks to the production of ever increasing quantities of the shiny white metal of which our nickels, dimes, quarters and

---

[138] The Constitution still directs this: "**Section 10.** No State shall enter into any Treaty, Alliance, or Confederation; grant Letters of Marque and Reprisal; coin Money; emit Bills of Credit; **make any Thing but gold and silver Coin a Tender in Payment of Debts;** pass any Bill of Attainder, ex post facto Law, or Law impairing the Obligation of Contracts, or grant any Title of Nobility."

dollars used to be made. By the end of the 19th Century, however, the silver/gold ratio had gone to 20:1. The decline in the real (as opposed to the official) value of silver, of course, slowly turned silver into the "bad money" which would then drive out the "good money", according to the relentless logic of Gresham's Law. The "good money", then became gold, which, as such, disappeared from the banking system and the vaults of the US Treasury as it became part of the private gold reserves of the more cautious private citizens who, whenever they saw economic storm clouds on the horizon began to feel the need of a golden safety blanket.

This desire of an anxious public to make gold unavailable for the money supply by removing it from their bank would not have mattered much if only the American economy had kept expanding, and the word "panic" could have been forever exiled to the history books. What happened instead, however, was that only twenty years after the economic crisis of 1873 an even bigger economic crisis came along. This was the "panic" of 1893. This was the economic and financial crisis that got financier J.P. Morgan out of his counting house and into his private railroad car headed for Washington, DC. The 1893 economic crisis was one of the more serious economic downturns of the 19th Century. On that occasion, however, the economic slowdown then lasted until the end of the 19th century.

The American Dollar Saved by Gold

221

Whether or not the basic bimetallic monetary migraines of 19th Century America were the principal cause of the economic crises that regularly occurred, is something that economic historians will continue to debate for some time to come. It is, however, entirely possible that it was the regular economic slowdowns that occurred throughout the century that caused the "panics" that occurred about every twenty years or so , rather than the other way around. In either case, after the "panic of 1873", and after the violent and destructive battles between railroad workers and national guardsmen that took place all over the country on that occasion, came the "panic of 1893." The economic crisis that struck in 1893 began at the end of a long lived and highly speculative bubble in railroad shares.[139] When the speculative frenzy around the railroads reached its peak the usual symptoms of mass financial hysteria presented themselves and were soon followed by bank runs, bank failures, crowds in the street, and the panoply of phenomena that accompanied each of the prior economic crises of 19th Century America. Thus, the widespread public fear of an unknown economic future led to massive withdrawals of gold and silver coinage from the banking system that so that the US dollar was once again placed in mortal danger.

---

[139] Beatty, Jack, *The Age of Betrayal: The Triumph of Money in America, 1865-1900*. New York: Alfred A. Knopf, 2007 is an excellently researched and extremely well written work largely devoted to the violent drama of 19th Century railroad finance, construction, and labor struggles that led up to the "panic" of 1893.

As the signs of a potentially deadly "panic" began to multiply in 1893, therefore, the tall, forceful, and patriarchically mustachioed J. P. Morgan strode dramatically onto center stage to save the US dollar, the New York financial community, and, of course, his own fortune. As the great financier sat confidently in his Washington D.C. hotel room awaiting a call from the President of the United States, a quick communication to the White House from the US Treasury unit stationed in New York City informed President Grover Cleveland that there were only $9 Million dollars in gold coins available to meet potential claims against US notes and bonds. The President sent for J.P. Morgan without further delay. When asked politely how he would propose to end the financial crisis, J.P. Morgan informed the President that he and his banking friends, the Rothschilds, could place three and a half million ounces of gold at the disposition of the US government in exchange for US bonds indicating repayment in gold after thirty years. This infusion of the magical yellow metal soon began to ease the mind of New York's financial community and, after a few more *coups de theatre*, the financial crisis began to die down.

The basic slowdown in the American economy, however, continued for some time after the stockbrokers and bankers of New York City had begun to relax. The traditional accounts of the "panic of 1893" tend to focus on more dramatic aspects of the crisis as it affected the New York banking and financial companies. Later treatments of US economic history in those years, however, seem to show that the financial crisis, which J.P. Morgan's last minute rescue brought to an end, occurred in the middle of a longer period of economic slowdown in which factories closed, banks failed, and working people were thrown out of their jobs throughout the United States. J.P. Morgan's exertions in the Oval Office in Washington, as well as his links to the Rothschilds, helped to end the financial crisis of 1893. The underlying economy, however, took the rest of the century to recover. What Morgan had done to save New York's financial world was to provide the required liquidity out of his own (and the Rothschild's) financial resources. This was exactly what a central bank would have done under similar circumstances, and what the Federal Reserve system has been trying to do in our own times. The basic lesson of the whole affair was not, however, so well understood in 1893. It would require another, and even more serious financial crisis, for both the financial community in New York and the national government in Washington to get the message about the need for a national central bank.

J.P. Morgan Teaches Uncle Sam How to Row Through Hard Times

Source: The United States Library of Congress

The following "panic" in 1907 was analyzed by a certain Mr. Noyes only a year or two after it took place. At that time Noyes set out the five factors that he believed could be used to identify a "panic of the first magnitude." These included: "a credit crisis"; a "general hoarding of money"; "financial helplessness"; "shutting down of manufacturing enterprises"; and, finally the "abrupt disappearance of buying demand throughout the country."[140] After applying these criteria, Noyes concluded that:

> The panic of 1907 was a panic of the first
>
> magnitude, and will be so classed in future economic
>
> history. Along with such financial episodes as the crises
>
> of 1893, 1873, 1857, and 1837.[141]

---

[140] Noyes, Alexander D., "A Year After the Panic of 1907", *The Quarterly Journal of Economics*, Vol. 23, No. 2 (Feb., 1909), pp. 185-212.
6. *Ibid.,p.186.*

While Noyes' list of factors certainly covers everything that happened during the 1907 economic crisis, what is probably more interesting about his remarks is Noyes' revelation to the effect that the American economy had the tendency to go into a severe crisis every twenty years or so. In his remarks on the subject, Noyes also reported that Andrew Carnegie had recently said that more modern methods of industry would speed up this cycle (the 1907 crisis came only 14 years after the previous one), but that "modern responses" would insure that such crises would also be more speedily resolved. This was not, however what happened.

The "panic of 1907" not only included several months of market turbulence created by an attempt of highly placed speculators to corner the market in the shares of copper companies, but also a general slowdown in the US economy that both preceded and survived the financial melodrama on Wall Street. The financial squeeze on Wall Street, on the other hand, resulted in the collapse of several banks and trust companies that had lent money to speculators involved in a highly dubious attempt to "corner" the copper market. Many banks were on the verge of failure on this occasion and one, the formerly highly regarded Knickerbocker Trust, actually failed. The high point of the financial maneuvers launched to prevent a complete meltdown of the system in 1907 occurred during one very long night time get together in J.P. Morgan's Park Avenue mansion. On this occasion, the legendary New York titan of finance locked some of New York's finest bankers into the library of his Park Avenue home until each and every one of them had pledged serious sums of money to be used to save the situation. The bankers' cash balances corralled by Morgan in this were was to be loaned to failing trusts and brokerage houses so as to prevent the imminent destruction of the New York City money market. Once again, J.P. Morgan had saved New York's financial community.

The "necessary funds" with which Morgan had prevented a complete meltdown of New York finance, needless to say, were all in the form of gold coins. When the shouting was over, and after Wall Street had narrowly escaped complete collapse, the Wall Street insiders began to ask each other what they would do in the next "panic" when J. P. Morgan was no longer there to save the day. The answer was, of course, that it was high time to create a national central bank.

The long and contentious process by which the creation of the Federal Reserve banking system of the United States was achieved began when five wealthy New York bankers traveled *incognito* to an obscure island off the coast of Georgia. Having left their top hats in Manhattan, the big bank conspirators traveled to Georgia disguised as a "hunting party" and spent several day long meetings creating the bankers' plan for a national central bank."[142] The whole project reached the level of

---

[142] For more interesting detail on this secret meeting see Ahamed, Liaquat,

national debate when discussion that the bankers had begun on Jekyll Island continued in the Congress of the United States.

The first proposals for creating a national central bank had been made by the very conservative and well connected Senate Republican Nelson Aldrich and his banker friends. This caused the opposing forces in the hundred year war over the American dollar to raise the old battle cries. Just as in Thomas Jefferson's and Andrew Jackson's day, rural and small town America and their representatives in Congress threw rhetorical cream pies at "Wall Street bankers." The debate continued for nearly five years.

Eventually, however, rational people on both sides of the barricades finally decided that a national bank was an absolute necessity in 20th Century America. When the report of the politically radical Pujo committee referred to the great "peril" to democracy constituted by the "money trust on Wall Street", however, Democratic voters all across the country rose as one to challenge the awesome power of money.

The Lords of Finance: The Bankers Who Broke the World, New York: Penguin, 2009, pp. 54-57.

The Panic of 1907 in Wall Street[143]

One result of this mobilization of the popular forces against the Wall Street bankers was that the Democrat Woodrow Wilson was elected President (1912). To make their point unanswerable, the voters also sent back a Democratic Congress to facilitate the job that, as a new President, Woodrow Wilson would have to face. Wilson was a conservative Democrat and, as such, might have been expected to share the wide spread popular fear and distrust of bankers. On the question of the proposed central bank, however, Wilson did not hesitate for a moment. Thus, the establishment of the Federal Reserve System (along with the establishment of the Federal income tax)

---

[143] Image sourced at: http://en.wikipedia.org/wiki/File:1907_Panic.png

during Wilson's administration went a long way towards creating the America that we live in today. The final legislation establishing the Federal Reserve was completed in 1913. This was also the year of J.P. Morgan's death which, along with the foundation of the national central bank that he had vigorously advocated, marked the end of an era.

The Federal Reserve Banking System

The long national debate over the necessity for and the necessary characteristics of a national central bank followed hard upon the heels of the economic disaster of 1907. Only two years after the "panic" of that year was over, a careful observer, Mr. O.W.M Sprague, launched his own suggestions for a national bank under the title of "The Proposal for a Central Bank in the United States: A Critical View."[144] While Mr. Sprague listed a number of good reasons for the creation of a national central bank, it is hard to find any "critical view" of the proposed institution in his essay. Noting that: "Dissatisfaction with the working of our credit machinery has become general", Sprague pointed out that "...on the occasion of severe financial strain it has almost invariably broken down with disastrous consequences to the entire business community."[145] In other countries, Sprague pointed out, "...central banks are the

---

[144] Sprague, O.M.W., "The Proposal for a Central Bank in the United States: A Critical View",
The *Quarterly Journal of Economics*, May 1910.
[145] *Ibid.*, p.364.

mainstay of credit in times of acute financial strain. Conservatively managed as they commonly have been, they have been able to lend freely in emergencies..."[146]

One of the main problems that Sprague foresaw for the establishment of a national central bank was the problem that might be created by the extensive physical area of the United States. To solve any of the difficulties of making economic policy that such great distances could cause, Sprague's 1909 article suggested, an effective national bank would have to have both a Federal and a regional component. When Sprague returned to his writing desk in 1913 to comment on the Federal Reserve Act that had just been passed, he found that he had most accurately predicted what the structure of the new national bank must look like, since both his regional and his Federal criteria had been satisfied.[147]

The most remarkable thing about the new Federal Reserve system set up in 1913 was that those on each side of the dollar war that had been going on in the United States for more than a century got what they wanted. The farmers, miners, and small businessmen of middle and far western states got regional banks. These were to be held in private hands and were created to offer guidance to regional bankers. On the other hand, the eastern big bank interest got Federal control of the banking

---

[146] *Ibid.*
[147] Sprague, O.M.W., "The Federal Reserve Act of 1913", *The Quarterly Journal of Economics*, Vol. 28, No. 2 (Feb., 1914), pp. 213-254

industry, and since they felt that they had achieved a satisfactory level of control over the Federal Government itself, they were very satisfied with the arrangement. In practice, however, Mr. Sprague's hope for regional and economic balance were not, in fact, truly realized. What happened instead was that the final outcome of the struggle to establish the Federal Reserve tended to benefit the big banks while imposing serious controls over the small ones. Thus, even while both sides of the century-long argument over money and banking got what they wanted, almost no one was really happy with the outcome.

The issue of trying once again to create an effective central bank for the United States had been so closely contested that, had it not been for a key political reversal by one of the most famous orator politicians in America, the Federal Reserve Act of 1913 might never have been passed. This famous orator was the oft-time presidential candidate and former "free silver" promoter William Jennings Bryan- the very same Congressman from Nebraska who had once pronounced in stentorian tones against the bankers' "cross of gold." After Bryan had finally given up his own presidential dreams, he had supported former Princeton President and 34th Governor of New Jersey, Woodrow Wilson, in the Democratic nominating convention of 1911. Bryan's reward came after Woodrow Wilson had won the presidential election of 1912, and William Jennings Bryan had been made Secretary of State. As Secretary of State in a Democratic administration, it was Bryan who talked the last

Democratic holdouts against the "bankers bill" out of their resistance to the idea of a national central bank and, at last, a new day had dawned.

The Federal Reserve today is structured more or less as the 1913 legislation decreed. It is comprised of twelve privately owned regional banks. These hold reserves that member banks in the region can call upon in emergencies. In this way, both regional interests and the traditions of private banking were satisfied by the creation of the Federal Reserve system. The system is, however, controlled and directed by the Board of Governors of the Federal Reserve which sits in Washington, DC. The Board of Governors is made up of the Chairman of the Board and seven Governors all of whom are appointed by the US President. The Chairman of "the Fed" serves a renewable term of four years, and is nominally independent of political control either from the White House or from Congress. At the time of its inception, the Federal Reserve's main reason for being was widely believed to be that of "lender of last resort" whenever the financial sector might begin to show signs of "panic."

This was, as in happened, a role which the Federal Reserve manifestly failed to play leading up to and after the 1929 of Black Friday stock market crash that kicked off a ten year economic crisis that was the worst that the American economy had ever experienced until then.[148] That lengthy and destructive crisis was baptized as the "Great Depression" rather than the "panic of 1929" for the simple reason that Herbert Hoover, who had the bad luck to be the US President at the time, thought that the term "panic" was too frightening. He thought that "depression" was a much less terrifying concept. By the early years of the 21st Century the phrase "Great Depression" was considered too frightening, and it was, accordingly, replaced with "Great Recession." In economics, it would appear, what you call it makes all the difference in the world.

Until the financial crisis that followed the bursting of the "housing bubble" in 2007, the normal business of The Federal Reserve was understood to be that of promoting a rate of economic growth consistent with stable prices. Under Board Chairman Alan Greenspan, who was the Governor of "the Fed" from 1987 until 2003, the Federal Reserve interpreted this mandate by moving quickly to increase the money supply during each and every period of economic crisis and stock market tension that occurred "on his watch." These occurred in 1987, 1991, 1998, and 2000. Greenspan's critics have since claimed that by simply pouring money on the problems that came up, the Governor of the Fed also managed to create massive amounts of excess liquidity in the US monetary system.

---

[148] Galbraith, J.K., *The Great Crash, 1929*, New York: Houghton Mifflin, 1972. See especially Chapter 3 "Something Should Be Done?", pp.28-47. For a more recent and more detailed account that features biographical information on some of the key players see Ahamed, *op.cit.*, pp.348-392.

This liquidity bubble, in turn, gave rise to no less than two major market bubbles during Greenspan's tenure as Governor of the Fed. These were the so-called "dot.com bubble" of the 1990s and the infamous "housing bubble" and the accompanying "sub-prime mortgage crisis" which began the last months of 2007 and early months of 2008. While the jury is still out on Greenspan's role in this matter, his successor, former Princeton Economics professor Ben Bernanke, has returned the Federal Reserve to its historic role, namely that of saving the banking and financial sector from its own fantasies and follies.

This is exactly what the Federal Reserve did during the "sub-prime mortgage crisis" of 2007-2008. That crisis resulted in the failure of a number of banks that had lent unwisely and unwell during the housing bubble that inflated effortlessly in the first few years of the 21st Century. When the "housing bubble" finally burst in the year 2007, a full scale disaster in financial markets was averted only with the assistance of "the Fed." This was done in much the same way that J.P. Morgan had saved the day with gold coins in 1893 and 1907. In 2008 the Federal Reserve, in conjunction with the US Treasury, treated a seriously unwell economy by injecting huge sums of money into the feverish giants of the financial sector. These included the following: the previously admired and respected Bank of America; the "household word" in American stock brokerage, Merrill-Lynch; and, finally even the once almighty American Insurance Group (AIG).

AIG had grown famously rich by selling financial derivatives called "credit default swaps." These almost impossible to understand financial instruments were widely touted as helping to "spread financial risk." It is now well known that AIG, an insurance company that had no real expertise in this field, made huge amounts of money in the "derivatives" markets by providing the newly rich financial organizations called "hedge funds" (about 8,000 of them) with the "securitization" that would allow them to place their bets on credit defaults in death defying leverage ratios at any where from 20:1 to 50:1.[149] These were the new derivatives that the dean of all investment managers, Warren Buffet, called "financial weapons of mass destruction." As far as Fed Chairman Bernanke is concerned, it must be said that he met with no small amount of criticism over his handling of the financial crisis that began in 2008, but it is likely that J.P. Morgan would have given the former Princeton professor a passing grade.

In more normal times the Federal Reserve system fulfills its mandate to maintain a regime of monetary stability consistent with economic growth by managing the US money supply. The tools that it uses to accomplish this task are as follows. To regulate the general rate of interest for bank loans throughout the economy, the Federal Reserve Board determines

---

[149] At 20:1 a single dollar controls 20 dollars worth of a contract, at 50:1 a single dollar controls 50 dollars worth of a contract. This is rewarding and fun when your bet pays off, and sheer hell when you are losing. To make things even more interesting, the one dollar in each case is usually borrowed money.

the rate of interest that the private banking sector must pay to borrow money by setting the so-called "rediscount rate." This is the rate of interest that banks who borrow from the Federal Reserve must pay. This technique may be used either to increase (by lowering interest rates) or to decrease (by raising interest rates) the money supply. The Federal Open Market Committee, which sits as part of the Federal Reserve Board in Washington, also engages in what are called "open market operations." These consist in the buying or selling of government bonds either to increase (by selling bonds) or to decrease (by buying bonds) the amount of money in circulation. Finally, the Fed also sets the so-called "reserve requirement." This expression refers to the ratio of each bank's monetary reserves to their outstanding loans. As part of its duty, the Federal Reserve may also make loans to troubled institutions in the financial sector as it did in conjunction with the US Treasury during the financial crisis of 2007-2008. A similar process was invoked to create funds for the $487 Billion economic stimulus package designed by the Obama Administration and applied from 2009 through 2010.

When the discussion comes to rest on the magic and the miracle that occurs when the Federal Government raises money, the question then becomes whether or not there any limit to the process whereby the Fed can create money by simply declaring that it exists. Can the Federal Reserve do this at the government's request without eventually risking the serious consequences of a runaway inflation? It is at this point that our discussion must return to the question of gold and it's relationship historic relationship to the money supply of the United States. If the current massive overhang of government deficits eventually results in a serious inflation (and the consequent decline in the value of the US dollar), then that would be the moment when gold would once again provide a "safe haven" type investment to protect the wealth of individuals and institutions during a time of monetary crisis. During the years from the creation of a new world monetary system at the Bretton Woods conference (1944), to the moment when US President Richard M. Nixon took the United States off the international gold system by "closing the gold window" at the US Treasury (1971), this question did not arise. A brief look at Bretton Woods and its monetary aftermath may tell us why.

Bretton Woods and the Dollar as International Money

What happens to the US dollar at the end of the first decade of the 21st Century is no longer a matter of concern for the US economy alone. The reason is that, following the Bretton Woods agreements of 1944, the US dollar became a truly international currency. What happened in the Mount Washington Hotel near Bretton Woods, New Hampshire in 1944 had never happened before. What emerged from that conference was a post-World War II monetary plan for no less than forty-four countries. The Bretton Woods agreement was proposed, debated, and agreed on after a period of weeks, and what it accomplished was to specify the exchange relationships of all of the national currencies involved with respect to the US dollar. The dollar itself was tied to gold at the Depression era level of $35 per ounce.

The conference was informally directed by the famous British economist, John Maynard Keynes, who used the last of his energies to establish a new monetary structure for the post war world. On this occasion, Keynes also proposed the creation of an international bank whose mandate would be that that of helping certain countries get back up on their feet. This was The World Bank which continues to play an important role in international economic development today. At the same time, Keynes proposed the creation of an international monetary reserve that would help countries in financial trouble to meet their payments to foreign creditors. This was the International Monetary Fund which has been similarly active in the realm of international economic affairs since that time.[150] Keynes suffered his last (of several) heart attacks on the way back to England after helping to negotiate a loan for the United Kingdom two years later. Shortly after his return from America, Keynes died at his home in Sussex on April, 21, 1946.

In his last contribution to the world of economic theory and practice, Keynes placed the mysterious yellow substance

---

[150] Wachtel, Howard, *The Money Mandarins*, New York: Pantheon, 1986.

that he had formerly referred to as a "barbarous relic" once again at the heart of the world monetary system. In the years that followed, the United States, as the only country that had not suffered the destruction of war on its national territory, used the dollar to rebuild the shattered economies of both of its enemies in World War II and those of its allies. In the years between 1944 and 1971, therefore, the dollar became the principal currency used in international trade. For this reason, the US dollar also became the international reserve currency. What this meant was that the central banks of other countries, and in particular those countries that were important US trading partners, held US dollars as a reserve against which to issue their own currencies. In short, during the immediate post World War II period the dollar was "as good as gold." This happy state of affairs lasted until after the United States had received the bill for the massive expense of the Vietnam War. The Vietnam War, it has been calculated, cost the United States (the range of estimates is wide) something between a conservative $113 Billion to a possible $400 Billion (both in 1975 dollars).

Whatever may have been the number entered on the famous "bottom line", the expenditure of lives and treasure in Vietnam had also exhausted both the supplies of gold on hand at the Treasury as well as international confidence in the US dollar. What followed the massive outflow of cash caused by the US expenditures in Vietnam was a slow but persistent "run on the bank" carried out by foreign nations. These were largely US

240

trading partners who had previously held dollars to back their currencies, but who now felt that they should exchange dollar credits for gold under the terms of the Bretton Woods agreement. When former General De Gaulle (1890-1970) was President of France (1959-1969), he was particularly insistent on presenting the US dollars that it had gained in trade for payment in gold at the US treasury. This action, taken together with De Gaulle's refusal to enlist French troops in NATO, resulted in a prolonged period of anti-French feelings among ordinary Americans.

As confidence in the dollar waned, however, America's other trading partners also began to repair to the US treasury to turn in their dollar balances for gold. Throughout the 1960s, therefore, the amounts of gold held by the US Treasury to meet demands for payment by US trading partners steadily declined. By the end of this period, US gold holdings had sunk to no more than 16% of the US dollars outstanding. To respond to this increasingly dangerous state of affairs, the US President, Richard Nixon not only decreed a "prices and incomes" policy for the US economy, but also unilaterally took the US out of the Bretton Woods agreements by "closing the gold window" of the US Treasury.[151]

This action, later called "the Nixon Shock", brought the Bretton Woods version of the gold standard for international

---

[151] A prices and incomes policy holds prices and wages constant and had not been used in the United States since the Second World War.

trade to a somewhat inglorious conclusion. It also made the US dollar the first international fiat currency ever. This was not, however, a situation that could be allowed to endure; the reason being that countries that engage in international trade tend to demand that the currency that they use should be backed gold. This was hardly strange since the "emperor" of the precious metals has played the dominant role in this respect throughout much of human history and trading nations have long memories in this respect. It was at this point in the story of the US dollar as the international reserve currency, however, that something new and different took place. What happened was that, despite the hemorrhage of gold from the US Treasury during and after the Vietnam War and even after the "Nixon shock", the US dollar went on to continue its role as an unquestioned and reliable international reserve currency for at least another thirty-five years. How did this happen?

There are two somewhat contrasting views on this point. One of these may be called "official view." The other may be called the "secret agreement view." Since the "secret agreement view" is both more logical and more interesting, let's begin with that one. The "secret agreement view" holds that shortly after President Nixon "shut the gold window of the Treasury" he, and his Secretary of State, Henry Kissinger, made a very interesting deal with King Faisal of Saudi Arabia. The "secret agreement" they made brought together the following factors: the latest in military hardware; the continued flow of crude petroleum at reasonable prices; and the role of the US dollar. According to the terms of this (still unpublished) agreement, the United States would provide the Saudis with both the latest and greatest in arms as well as with military protection. All the Saudi Royal family had to do to secure this favor was to agree to accept only the US dollar in payment for their apparently infinite supplies of petroleum.

This agreement was made just before the eruption of the second Arab Israeli war (1973) and the Organization of Petroleum Exporting Countries (OPEC) boycott that followed the beginning of hostilities. The OPEC "boycott" caused gasoline shortages all across the United States, and in most European countries as well in the 1973-4 period. Nevertheless, the petroleum sales that continued during this period and, indeed, petroleum sales down to the present day were/are all priced in US dollars. What the American President and his Secretary of State appear to have accomplished in their agreement with the Saudis, then, was nothing less than to end the US dollar's brief existence as an international fiat currency.

Now, the dollar would be implicitly backed by the one commodity that all the developed nations of the world wanted at all times and in ever increasing quantities- namely petroleum. [152] The official view of the matter, on the other hand, explains

---

[152] See Adask, Alfred, "The Petrodollar is About Out of Gas", *Adask's Law.* Available online at:

the continued strength of the US dollar as an international reserve currency by saying that : " ... the oil producing countries, notwithstanding their hostility toward the United States, stayed with their practice of accepting only dollars for payment- not yen, not marks, not gold, only dollars." [153]   The "hostility" mentioned here, of course, refers to the world turmoil occasioned by the Arab Israeli war of 1973 and the OPEC oil boycott that followed. These events raised international oil prices by a factor of four.   It is quite amazing, therefore, that in the middle of warfare, international boycotts, and growing tension between the Middle Eastern countries and the United States, the dollar remained the only currency that could be exchanged for crude oil anywhere in the world. In other words, if you had enough dollars in your bank account you could always purchase a tanker full of oil, and someone would always be willing to buy it from you. Whether or not this occurred as the result of quiet conversations between Nixon and Kissinger and the Saudi Royal family, or as the result of the petroleum countries continuing to do business in the same old way, the US dollar retained its unquestioned international role until the end of the 20th Century and for the first few years of the 21st Century as well.

---

http://adask.wordpress.com/2010/01/12/the-petro-dollar-is-almost-out-of-gas/.
See also: Sharma, Sohan, Tracy, Sue, and Kumar, Surinder, "The Invasion of Iraq: Dollar v. Euro", *Z Magazine*, (February, 2004). Available online at: http://www.thirdworldtraveler.com/Iraq/Iraq_dollar_vs_euro.html
[153] Wachtel, *Op.Cit.* , p. 86.

However, several potent factors may now threaten the dollar's international role. These are: the advent of an expensive war in Iraq (2003); an endlessly growing US military commitment in Afghanistan (2010); the cost of maintaining US military bases in more than 400 countries around the world; and, the major world wide economic crisis which began late in 2007 and which by 2010 had not yet come to an end. Under these conditions, it does not require a great deal of imagination to see that eventually the international role of the dollar could be seriously challenged at some point in the future. In addition to these global realities we should probably also bear in mind the following domestic concerns:

- the declining tax revenues associated with an ongoing economic slowdown
- ever increasing domestic and foreign trade deficits
- the massive American debt to China of more than $2Trillion along with a similar amount owed to Japan.

Taking all of the above factors into consideration, it might appear that the international rule of dollar could, one day, come to a close. Certainly, one of America's biggest trade partners, China, seems to think this might be case. Accordingly, the Chinese government added gold to their financial reserves as mentioned earlier. What the decline of the dollar, if and when it happens, may mean for both individuals and institutions is that simply that acquiring a certain amount of gold as insurance against downside risk would be a good idea. The list of those who might wish to consider this possibility includes those who might simply decide to put some of their dollars into gold physicals. It also includes those who would like to balance their portfolios with shares in gold mining companies (or a gold based ETF) against a possible decline of the dollar. Finally, there are also those who might even see the possibility of the profit to be gained by speculation in gold markets. In short, things may very well come to pass such that the magic mystery metal, gold, shall once again come to play the role of "safe haven" investment and/or speculative opportunity.

We have reached the end of our story. Unlike many economists, the author of this account of the long history of gold and money does not imagine that it is possible to see into the future. What lies ahead for the US dollar and for your savings may be stated only in terms of probabilities. These will be very briefly noted in the "After Word" that follows.

Afterword

No one can foresee the future, not even economists. The best we can do in an honest way is to point to probabilities. In times gone by, pointing to probabilities meant assuming the familiar Gaussian distribution first, concluding that unusual outcomes would be located out in the extreme ends of the distribution , and assuming that they would be small in number. Now economists, statisticians, and financial writers like to talk about "fat tails." The "tails" referred to in this expression are the "tails" of the Gaussian normal distribution. In these times, it would appear, there are many more unanticipated outcomes lurking out there four and five standard distributions from the mean. Even if true, this would not relieve economists, policy makers, financial writers and others of the task of looking at the probable play of economic forces in future markets. Where, more specifically, the value the US currency is concerned, we should probably consider (at least) the following four things that could affect the fate of the dollar in probabilistic terms: 1) the ravages of inflation; 2) ill considered government spending; 3) expensive wars; and, 4) the economic fears engendered by sovereign defaults.

What inflation means for individuals and families is that prices go up faster than incomes, and that the dollar loses its ability to provide consumers with what they have enjoyed in the past. If the moderate inflation experienced in the US at most times since the end of World War II were to be accelerated by an exceptional level of government spending, by the expense of war, or by more "bailouts" for the financial community a merely "moderate inflation" could become a "runaway inflation." Such an inflation would, of course, be welcomed by debtors, would be anathema to creditors, and, more importantly, could destroy the savings, retirement portfolios, and economic security of everyone else.

Under the heading of government spending, the first decade of the 21st Century saw two expensive wars, a dramatic rescue of the financial sector, and large economic stimulus intended to bring a languishing US economy back to life. Whether one should agree or disagree with the necessity and/or wastefulness of such government outlays of money is not what we are concerned with here. What is crucial, however, is whether or not government spending shall reach a point that will accelerate inflation to "runaway" levels. If and when this happens, there will not be many safe harbors. A certain amount of gold ownership can be one of those safe harbors.

Finally, in our probabilistic look into the future there is the possibility of fear. When a sovereign country defaults on its debts, there are large numbers of people who suddenly fear that sovereign defaults could bring down the entire international financial system and various national currencies with it. This type of fear will, most probably, continue to have a strong effect on the price of gold. There is also the fear of war. War in the

Middle East, however, could have the additional effect of cutting off important energy supplies. Fear of this kind has already lifted the gold price well over a thousand US dollars. These are the probable causes of serious economic disruption and change that could occur in a not far distant future. The facts and history of gold and money have been presented here with a view towards suggesting ways to protect your wealth and your security if some

of the above probabilities become realities. The rest is up to you.

www.ingramcontent.com/pod-product-compliance
Lightning Source LLC
Chambersburg PA
CBHW070550130626
46556CB00001B/98